# Cocky Duke

## SARA FORBES

ISBN-13: 978-1542651196
ISBN-10: 1542651190

# ACKNOWLEDGMENTS

Thanking the people who cheered me on and gave me priceless feedback: SusieQ, Kathleen Rovner, Marisa Wright, Debby Wallace, Jhawk, Robin and Alix. Also my editor, Claire, and writing guru, Tammi, and my ever-wonderful cover designer, Neptunian. And finally, the awesome Sterling&Stone guys and all the apprentices.

# 1

HAYLEY

Two weeks touring art galleries in London—that's what my Uncle Stig promised. A nice quiet trip with my favorite relative. The only problem? It's a little *too* quiet. I crave something more than four o'clock tea and crumpets. Which is how I ended up here, at *Jayvee's* nightclub.

Not a soul has spoken to me since I arrived an hour ago. Not even after my energetic stint on the dancefloor. It goes to prove how exclusive this VIP section is, if the polished teak, starched shirts, and stiff laughter didn't already make it obvious. Or maybe all London clubs are like this, I don't know. I'm from Laxby, Oregon, population: 2514, and we don't do nightclubs.

Halfway through my second Cosmopolitan, a man's grumbling interrupts my thoughts, but it's just the bartender losing his shit. I peer over the bar and see the problem—a dome of froth billowing out of a cocktail glass. The barman growls again. "Why the hell does everyone want *Cuba Reales?* This damn thing is broken."

I recognize the problem right away. His soda gun is getting too much gas. It's a faulty valve. This sometimes happens with my airbrush back home. I open my mouth to explain, but he's bent down, tugging at the connection to the regulator.

"Don't do that!" I plant my butt on the bar, swing my legs over, and yank his arm off the connector. The $CO_2$ leak probably wouldn't kill us, but I hate to see equipment manhandled like this.

"Trying to poison us?"

He looks unsure.

"The pressure's too high." I eke an opening in the valve and watch the needle lower to 280 psi. I straighten, hot faced.

My heroics have drawn attention from a bunch of supermodels lounging in a nearby alcove, their faces contorted in horror—or amusement, it's hard to tell which.

The barman grabs up the soda gun. "Now scram, American girl."

"Excuse me?"

He draws an air rectangle, indicating his domain behind the bar. "Staff only."

When I don't react, he says, "What do you want? A medal?"

I straighten my T–shirt. "A simple thanks would do." Whatever happened to the famous British politeness?

"Leave your number. We can hook up. Isn't that what you call it?"

I refuse to dignify that with an answer.

He inspects the nozzle. "Better not have broken it." Pressing the trigger, he gets his answer—soda blasts toward me, zaps my chest, soaks my T–shirt.

I shriek.

With a faintly apologetic look, he hands me a wad of napkins. I shoot him my meanest look, which I've been told looks adorable, but it's all I got.

Back on my bar stool, I hunch over my drink. He continues with the now perfectly shooting soda gun. All it needed was my tweak to that valve. I force myself to focus on higher matters—the galleries I want to visit tomorrow, day two of my two–week stay, my plans for world domination—but it's hard to concentrate. The supermodels are jittery. They swing their blonde tresses petulantly and giggle loudly. What, seriously, is their problem?

Within seconds, I notice a flash of white in my periphery. I slide my gaze down the bar and I almost laugh. Correction, I *do* laugh, but it comes out more like a whimper.

To say the man in the gleaming white shirt is handsome is a disservice to him. His is a beauty perfected by centuries of selective breeding, perfect bone structure, luscious dark hair, a broad plane of a forehead, straight insolent nose, luminous skin. And the eyes ... they're arresting. He's the kind of model I dream of encountering in my life–drawing class—a joy to sketch. And if he's not a billionaire of some kind with his expensive suit, heavy red gold watch, and glistening shoes, then I'm not an impoverished art student in a soda–soaked T–shirt.

I'm about average in looks—could be better, could be worse—five pounds overweight, depending on who you ask, and I've accomplished nothing yet. He's so far out of my league, I wouldn't find him with the Hubble telescope. If he comes an inch closer, I'll run.

I shut my eyes and let the negativity pass. When I reopen them, he's draped his blazer over the stool between us, which, as any anthropology student will tell you, means he's marking territory. But I'm pretty sure that when he has the cream of the crop at his disposal, he wouldn't go for someone like me, so this is just some game to pass the time or to lure the models out of their cozy corner.

A cocky smirk etches a groove across his perfect jaw. I whip my gaze away.

"Gin. Tanqueray," he says to the barman.

I love his commanding baritone voice. His clipped accent is one degree of snobbery away from the Queen herself, calling to mind aristocracy dramas on the BBC. Seriously, I didn't know people still talked like this. Even in Britain.

The barman hunts among bottles on a shelf for the correct gin. Then he stands frozen with the soda gun aimed at Mr. Model. Is our hapless barman going for a double strike?

"Lemon and tonic, sir?"

"Sir?" Mr. Model repeats. He gives the barman the briefest of once-overs. "You're new."

"First day, sir." The barman laughs nervously. "Uh, lemon and tonic?"

Mr. Model's gaze flickers to my soda-soaked chest. "Neither. Cucumber and ice, if it's not too much trouble."

I roll my eyes and pour the last of the Cosmopolitan down my dry throat. As much as Dad's meekness gets on my nerves, I'm not overly fond of his opposite either—entitled jerks, full of power, money, and themselves. From hanging around with Uncle Stig, I've met quite a few like that. I bet Mr. Cucumber's day consists of jet-setting, networking, Michelin-starred dining, late night socializing in clubs like this, then Michelin-starred fucking. He'll take one of those supermodels home tonight and disappear tomorrow into thin air. And yet, I'm riveted to him with the same fascination I'd have for a wolf with brilliant, ice-blue eyes.

"Hi."

The vision has spoken. To me, apparently.

"Oh." My heart gallops off, my brain lagging far behind. "Hi."

"You're also new." His gaze slides over me and I get the sense he's already slotted me neatly into some category far down the food chain.

I clear my throat. "Yeah, just over from the US. I've been looking at the art today."

He nods. "Hard to fit it all in in one day, don't you think?"

"Not least because eighty percent of it's in storage," I shoot back.

His wolf eyes widen a fraction and conduct a more leisurely tour of my T-shirt and then my face. "Are you cold?"

"I'm fine." I put down my empty glass for emphasis. And then I have no clue what to say.

"Nice rescue action." He tilts his glass at me, like he's Jay Gatsby or something, and raises it to his bountiful lips.

"Oh, you saw that?" I flick my gaze meaningfully to the barman and back. "He was all gratitude. He even offered to hook up with me." I don't know why I'm sharing this with him.

Mr. Cucumber's gaze as it meets mine is intense and steady. "Is that your best offer tonight?"

"It's the best so far."

He inhales deeply, filling out his broad chest, making the shirt peel back a little more to expose hints of dark chest hair. My fascination with his beauty is no longer academic—I've an urge to slip my hand inside the shirt, to hold my palm flat over his pecs, smooth my hands down the gym–honed muscles, making them tighten for a moment. I want to feel a perfect body like his on top of mine, beneath mine, beside mine, inside mine, before I go and carry on with the rest of my normal life.

I brazenly hold his gaze as I pick up my glass, but then I remember the damn thing is empty, so I put it down again. I search around for another prop. If this was an old eighties movie, I'd light up a cigarette and blow a smoke ring in his face. For now, all I can do is clasp my hands around my knee.

He raises his left index finger an inch away from his glass and cocks his head. The barman zooms over so fast I'm beginning to wonder if Mr. Cucumber here is the owner of this joint.

"Fill her up," he says to the barman.

I cringe. But his face betrays no signs of having meant it suggestively. When the barman hands me a new Cosmopolitan, I accept, saying, "Thanks, you came a lot faster than I expected."

The barman throws me a dour glance and goes away.

A smile tugs at the edge of Mr. Cucumber's lips, causing a cross between a dimple and a laugh line to indent his perfectly stubble–covered cheek. I feel ridiculously happy to have earned this much from him.

His beautiful eyes narrow to lines of dark lashes. "I hope your expectations are not too low."

"Regarding?" In a fatalistic way, I want to see where this is heading. Whether, in theory, he'd be interested in someone like me. I might learn something about flirting with the British upper class, although I can't imagine what. I think my uncle purposely got my name onto this VIP list because he reckoned I'd never manage to pick anyone up here.

"Regarding your offers for tonight."

"I'm open to suggestions," I say, lifting my gaze brazenly to meet his.

"As am I." His grin is wicked. "Watching your skirt flying as you leapt over the counter to fix that gas leak or whatever it was, was very suggestive. And, should I say, most welcome. Not to mention the Hello Kitty knickers."

Heat seeps into my cheeks. "Yeah. I really didn't expect to be showing those to anyone tonight."

His glass hovers at his mouth. "Bottoms up." He polishes off the cucumber gin in one gulp, presses those gorgeous lips together and looks at me, waiting.

"How has today treated you?" I ask out of a sudden desire to keep this conversation alive.

"It's been interesting." He swivels the bar stool to face me directly, legs stretched in front of him, crossed at the ankles. My feet dangle in the air and I force myself to stop swinging them. I wonder what the height difference would be between us if we were both to stand up. "But information has a price."

My skin prickles. Is he propositioning me? God, if he could hear my heartbeat, it would so betray me. He'd know how fired up I am about the thought of touching him, let alone doing something mercenary in exchange for information.

He gets up and drapes his blazer across my shoulders, trapping in what little heat is there. I relish the way his fingers graze the nape of my neck, making my hairs stand on end. A line has been crossed.

"Name your price." There, it's out. I said it.

"Your name would be a start," he says. "And your number."

"Sure." I've got nothing to lose giving him my number. It's a temporary SIM card for this trip only. I'll never use it again after I return home in two weeks.

"Here." He slides a coaster toward me, and without warning, leans in and reaches inside his blazer, his fingers mere inches from my chest. He smoothly produces a pen from a hidden inner pocket and hands it to me. I uncap it carefully, focusing on not dropping it and ruining my act of nonchalance. It's a fountain pen. Heavy, gold–plated. The Cartier logo catches my eye. As I jot down my name and number, they glide out in silky blue ink.

*Who are you?* He can't be a banker or doctor—they don't make so much so young. He's dressed too conservatively to be a tech entrepreneur. An industry mogul, perhaps? Or the son of one. He looks too young to have built up an empire by himself. His complexion suggests time spent outside, in the sun, in the wind—as opposed to in an office. Although the ruggedness adds a few years to his appearance, he's still only mid–twenties, not more than four or five years older than me.

He's reading the coaster. "Thanks ... Hayley."

I like the sound of my name from his lips.

Glancing around, I realize we've built up quite an audience. People are either staring blatantly at us or they're huddled, whispering about us. We seem to outrank the celebs in the corner because they're all watching us. I swivel back to him. It's time I asked him who he is and stuff, although it feels like an intrusion on the cozy atmosphere of mystery we've got going on.

He draws closer, pushing aside the in–between stool. This is not the kind of place where they nail stools to the floor. His body blocks my view of the prying eyes, enveloping me inside his cocoon of attention, so close I could touch his hand if I let my arm flop down. But I don't. I wait for him to say something, relishing the close–up view of his luminous skin and the intoxicating aftershave, musky with blackcurrant top notes.

"You want to know what else happened today? Apart

from meeting you?" He flicks the coaster between his fingers. "So, let's see. Before I came here, Ken and I—Ken, my brother—we went to a dinner over in the Overseas League, an annual affair. We had lamb." He winces. "Always lamb."

"Can't stand it either," I say, laughing.

He grins back and my heart warms another few degrees. "After pudding, I got involved in a bit of a standoff with a certain dignitary. Are you telling me you haven't seen this on social media yet?" He pulls out his phone from his pants pocket.

I shake my head. Am I supposed to know who this guy is?

"See for yourself." He holds up his phone. It's YouTube. I lean in to follow the video.

"He started it. He had the gall to suggest that our dealings in the Middle East were suspect. Talk about the pot calling the kettle. Well, I put him straight."

I grab the earbuds he's offering and shove them in my ears. My eyes and ears greedily absorb the details of the scene. Mr. Cucumber is sitting at a lavish banquet with another sickeningly handsome guy beside him, same looks, but blond, who can only be his brother. Someone off camera is addressing him. "And what does the Duke of Fernborough say to this?"

*Duke? This guy's a duke?*

"Well, if Mr. Lawson is so worried about our family dealings, I suggest he refocus some of that apprehension on his own cronies' affairs."

My heart gives a sickening lurch when I hear "Lawson." Around the banquet table, hands fly to mouths, just as mine is doing now. I lean in closer to the phone. Cameras flash as the duke continues to argue. He can't shut up and makes it worse as he talks more and more—and more. Blond guy's squirming, yanking his sleeve, telling him to shut the fuck up.

A familiar roar sounds: "Do you know who you're talking to?" to which the duke smoothly replies, "Absolutely, Mr. Ambassador. Having diplomatic immunity has turned you into a first-grade asshole."

And then with a jerk of the camera, the video's over. It has 374,857 hits. Posted forty–five minutes ago. I scroll up and read the title. "Cocky Duke Offends US Ambassador!"

I yank out the earbuds, slam them back onto the bar beside the phone. I pull off his blazer and throw it back on the stool. I scoot as far away from him as my body will go without falling off the barstool. "Did you hit him?"

He brushes imaginary lint off his blazer. "Of course not."

"Hurt him in any way?"

"No."

"You insulted him enough, though."

"He deserved it." His grin returns at half wattage.

In a flash of white rage, I lift my full Cosmopolitan and throw it over him. "Nobody insults my Uncle Stig!"

I take a moment to enjoy the look of incomprehension written on his perfect face. I'd actually been aiming for that. But his soaking crotch is a satisfying outcome too. I leap off the stool and stomp the hell out of there.

2

ALEX

"Why, Alex? Why, why, *why?*" Ken shoves the iPad across the desk toward me. I don't have to rise from the depths of my leather chair to see what site he's on. Instead I loll my head back against the headrest, letting the silence draw out whatever grievance he has with me.

The study is still crammed with Father's books and some of his more recent art acquisitions that nobody knows quite what to do with. Ken's been holing himself up here writing a book on his most successful racehorse, *Silmarillion*, although I suspect he spends more time surfing. I normally only ever come here to pour myself a gin from the collection—Father's hardly going to complain now—and to enjoy the unspoiled panorama of leather, gold, and parkland. But this morning before breakfast, Ken said he wanted "a word" in a quiet place. So here we are.

He's raking his hands through his hair, making it stand up like some surfer boy's. Something tells me little brother's picking a fight. Or maybe he just wants reassurance. But even if he were to ask nicely, I have none to give.

"Was bashing the ambassador not good enough for you for one night? No, you had to go and produce a goddamn sequel."

I put down my mug of coffee on a free patch of desk and flex my fingers. "Steady on, I didn't know she was his *niece.*"

He emits a groan as if my incredible stupidity has landed a punch in his gut. Ken would have made a great actor, an effortless Hamlet. "You must've known she was *somebody.* She was in *Jayvee's.* The *VIP* section. Couldn't you have at least found out before you opened your big gob?"

I stare him down.

His head shakes furiously. "Words fail me, Alex."

"Good, then maybe you'll shut up about it."

I rise, conduct a slow semicircle of the space in front of the desk, and end up leaning my elbow against the marble mantelpiece. My great–grandfather's portrait scowls down at me more sternly than usual this morning. Of course, *now* I know her name is Hayley Cochrane, niece of US ambassador Stig Lawson. According to YouTube, a further three hundred thousand people know who she is. The clip of her dumping her drink over my crotch has eclipsed the one of me insulting the US ambassador—her *uncle.*

The growing YouTube audience is enthralled by Hayley Cochrane and what she represents—the spunky commoner showing it to the wastrel aristocrat. They've even given her a nickname—Duchess Wet T-Shirt. I wonder how she's handling her sudden fame. She'll be endorsing products herself next. Cosmopolitans, maybe? Or knickers. If we ever meet again, those are coming off.

Someone in the club had a high–end camera trained on us the entire time. They captured the look of innocence on her pretty little face at that moment I handed her my phone. I'm not complaining—they also captured her curves underneath the damp T–shirt and her hard nipples jutting through the wet cotton.

"What's Mother going to say?"

I jab my finger at Ken's chest. "Let me talk to her *before* she sees the videos and someone else tells her what to think."

"Fine." Ken yanks up his towel that's been on the seat beside him. I hope he manages to thrash out all his

11

frustrations against his beloved punching bag in the downstairs gym because I, for one, am starting to dislike the size of his biceps.

Hand on the door handle, he adds, "This would never have happened if Seb were here."

"Well, he's not."

The look he throws me is as withering as any Mother could muster up.

"You know what, Alex? I don't care anymore. It's your life. You want to waste time on flying your helicopters and wining and dining as if nothing's happened, then do that. But don't draw attention like this. The public hates us enough already."

"I've put pilot school plans on hold," I reply. It's a travesty, but something had to give. My flying instructor, Mike, looked devastated under his stoic mustache when I broke the news to him yesterday. I tried to sound convinced that it wouldn't be forever, but he wasn't buying it. Even Molly, his Irish setter, looked sad. That nearly killed me. I suppose it's what drove me to ruffle Lawson's feathers later on.

"On hold?" Ken scratches his jaw. "For how long?"

"Indefinitely." The word escapes through my gritted teeth.

"That's something. But Seb had better come back soon. You're clearly not fit to run the estate." Ken strides to the door and slams it behind him.

Given his cavalier age of twenty–three, I'll cut him some slack. He was Father's favorite—Father, who was supposed to live forever so we'd never have to deal with this bullshit. At this moment, I'd do *anything* to change the inheritance rules. Primogeniture has ruined my life. Because let's face it, Seb, Ken, and Letty would all be better candidates for the title and responsibilities of duke than me. Especially Seb, who's oldest and always has been the responsible one.

I pull out my phone to call Marty. I've three missed calls from him. Marty's an MI6 operative of vague job description. He did tell me the exact title that one time he was drunker than me, but I forget what it was. We've been best friends since our Charterhouse school days when I rescued the scrawny, curly–headed seven–year–old from bullies twice our size. That's my version, anyway, and I'm sticking to it.

"I googled her," I tell him by way of greeting. I never have to explain context with him. As heir to an earldom himself— albeit a scrappy one—he shares the concerns and constraints of my entitled world. He's my joker card. Every duke should have one.

"Yeah," Marty says in his I've–been–up–six–hours voice. "Art student from Oregon and niece of the ambassador. It checks out. No criminal record. Nothing to see there, but—"

"Plenty to see on the video, though. Did you get a load of that?"

There's a telling pause on Marty's side. "The uncle. He's a piece of work."

"Well, one is quite aware of that."

"Alex, we all know Stig Lawson's not above a bribe or three, but thanks to your little tiff with him, some operatives in our internal affairs division started poking deeper. The cronyism you alluded to in your Oscar–winning speech yesterday is spot on, but it's just the tip of iceberg."

"What iceberg? He's the US ambassador to Britain, for Chrissakes."

"Just listen. This is important. Last month two Azerbaijanis met him in secret and bribed him to push concessions their way during the trade talks in Vienna last week. We think it's oil tycoons trying to smooth their way into the British market. Well, for whatever reason, belated guilt, who knows, Lawson flaked on them. I guess he figured they'd just forget about it because he hadn't taken their money. But our sources tell us these tycoons are *seriously* pissed off and could be planning to top him off in case he's some kind of spy for some other oil company."

"What?"

"Yeah, our government knows everything, but wants to avoid an international incident. They certainly don't want a

dead ambassador on their hands. I should congratulate you—
we wouldn't have been alerted to this at all without your
media splashes. Someone in MI5 was checking up on whether
your slander had any basis or not and stumbled on the
Azerbaijani meetings. You just made our job easier for once."

"Glad to be of service." I shake my head at the stupidity
of the ambassador. Did I just stick my foot in a hornet's nest
way bigger than I thought?

"And now, since your YouTube vignette, the Azerbaijanis
are aware of his niece being here and she may be an alternate
target. We could use your help."

"*My* help? Why?"

"You've had contact with her. Don't you think it strange
that she shows up in your Friday night haunt straight after
you insult her uncle?"

"Marty, I've long given up trying to figure out the people
in Jayvees."

"She might've been looking for help."

I hate having to think this early in the morning. If I do
exert my mental faculties before nine, it's only ever to
remember the name of the women wriggling under my
sheets. I'm starting to feel grumpy. "She's got a funny way of
asking for help. And she didn't seem to even *know* who I was.
Unless she's a great actress, and I haven't quite banished that
thought from the realm of possibility."

"Either way, they're slated to fly back to the States
tomorrow—there's been a flight re-booking early this
morning—but that's a bad idea. They'll have no protection
over there, whereas here we're watching them like hawks."

My mind is whirling. "But they have full diplomatic
immunity."

Marty laughs. "You think these oil tycoons give a shit?
They're criminals."

I picture her innocent face, her rosy, apple cheeks, the
glint of goodness in her clear, hazel eyes. She didn't seem the
type to go to such lengths to attract the interest of secret
services, if that's what she was doing. But it wouldn't be the

first time I've been deceived by a woman's looks. And I suppose it demonstrates great loyalty to her uncle even if the net result is to potentially land them both in danger. It's a delicious irony with a bitter aftertaste. She doesn't deserve this. Underneath my budding curiosity, a familiar companion is clawing for attention: guilt.

"*If* I call her, I need complete privacy, Marty. Can you block her phone from the rest of the spooks so they can't snoop?"

He laughs uneasily. "Not if I want to keep my job."

I remain silent. Marty just needs a few moments to think and then he'll come around. He's never refused me. I still remember the day after receiving our exam results, a lecturer sliding up and asking him if he wanted to do "something stimulating" in the foreign service. I told him it sounded like fun, so he went for it and he's been there ever since. In another life, I might have been a career guidance counselor.

"Come on. If she's in danger, I should warn her what Uncle Scumbag's really mixed up in because I truly don't think she knows."

Marty sighs. "Fine. But no messing around."

"What do you mean?" I ask coolly.

"She's not your usual type, okay? Uncle may be the ambassador but she's a nobody from Nowhereville, Oregon. Father's a simple law–abiding fisherman. Mother's dead."

"He'll be happy to get his darling daughter back then," I reason, and I read out the number from the coaster.

Hope Duchess Wet T–Shirt doesn't mind being woken early.

# 3

## HAYLEY

Bzzzzz!

The phone vibrates in my front jeans pocket. It feels angry. We're up to twenty–three ignores now. I know who it is. He's the only person other than Dad, Uncle Stig, and Mara who has my phone number. But what does he want? I'm so not in the mood for this.

It's a soggy morning. Yes, not only am I a newly–minted porn star in Britain—or as the YouTube comments would have it "Duchess Wet T–Shirt"—but Uncle Stig's had a hissy fit over my behavior and has decided we have to fly back to Portland *tomorrow* to avoid the situation getting worse.

No amount of arguing would make him change his mind. His secretary had already changed the flights. I sure as hell don't have the money to hang around London on my own. So, my patched–together plan of visiting the National Portrait Gallery and the Tate all in one day is the best I can do to salvage something of this trip. With less than thirty hours left in the country, I'm not going to waste one second of them dealing with *His Grace*.

Yup, the correct term of address for a duke is apparently "Your Grace." Another interesting fact from Wikipedia. I wonder if anyone actually calls him that.

As London's art institutions infuriatingly take until 10 a.m. to wake up, Uncle Stig and I have wandered past Buckingham Palace, down Birdcage Walk toward the Imperial War Museums. There's a small independent gallery in some alleyway around there called Smithfield that actually opens at 8:30.

"Sooner we're home, the better, Hayley." Uncle looks up from his phone. He's multi–tasking as we stroll and seems jittery as hell, often muttering to himself. "Give it all a chance to die down."

I nod, but Uncle Stig, of all people, must know that hundreds of thousands of YouTube hits don't simply die down. They stay there forever, attracting new views with every generation. He's got several thousand of his own to contend with. My one consolation is that Dad hasn't seen the video yet. He'd have called me first thing if he had. But it's only a matter of time before some gossiping neighbor lets him know.

As for me, it doesn't matter how much art I'll ever produce over the next decades because I'll never be more famous for anything than for those five seconds in which I poured a Cosmopolitan over a British duke's crotch. It's partly the reason I refuse to answer the phone.

I've got several theories as to why the duke might be calling me. He probably thinks I feel sorry for what I did, now that I've found out how exceedingly important he is. He thinks I want to atone and he'll play with that for sure. Well, guess what? He can pay his own dry–cleaning bill, because I'm not answering.

"Uncle Stig, what's a duke? I mean, what do you have to do to become a duke?"

My uncle snorts. "There's only one way, and that's by being the oldest son of a duke, and having your father die, as his did, last month. Rather unexpectedly, if the accounts are to be believed."

The duke's twenty–six, according to Google. That seems early to lose a dad. Of course, parents can go at any age, as I well know.

"Although," Uncle Stig continues, "he'd have had the benefits of being a duke even before he gained the title."

"Like what?"

"Apart from being heir to a ridiculously large estate and castle and somehow related to the Windsors? Well, there's the access to the top jobs in banking, politics, memberships to exclusive clubs, British Airways black frequent flyer cards—that's the level above gold. He'd also have courtesy titles, like Earl of this, Viscount of that. I believe there's a page full of his secondary titles. Of course, now that he's duke, those extra titles are just added fluff."

Uncle Stig eyes me before continuing. "More practically, he'd get preferential treatment in restaurants, get seated with no reservations, that type of thing. And he'd get special service in banks, and high–end shops. No queues for this guy. He ranks higher than every minister, every envoy, bishop or member of the peerage in the land apart from his twenty–two fellow dukes. He can date whoever he wants—actresses and models usually, and has a high chance of marrying a foreign royal. Need I go on?"

"That's okay, thanks, Uncle Stig." I turn my head to examine the patterns on the gates of James Park so I don't appear too keen for information.

We totter along another half mile or so in silence until we reach the chipped painted gallery entrance adorned with a hand–scrawled sign demanding a five–pound entrance fee. We loiter in the doorway to get out of the drizzle more than from any great enthusiasm to see the exhibits.

Uncle Stig shakes out his umbrella. "As long as the British continue to treat people as special on the basis of their birth, then they'll have some kind of aristocracy. Note it well, my dear, because the art world's a popular resting place for the idle dukes and earls of this world."

"Yeah, I guess they have money and time to spare."

He nods. "And it's all about connections. It doesn't matter if you have no talent whatsoever, because if you can get noticed by the right agents, galleries, and buyers, then you're in the game."

I take a promotional brochure from a wire rack and pretend to study it, because I need to bolster myself against Uncle Stig's gamification of everything I'm working hard for. I came here to immerse myself in art for two weeks, to give myself a huge advantage in my new semester at college. I'd have notebooks crammed with sketches and ideas for new directions with my paintings and dissertations. I didn't mind my uncle vetting where I went at night so long as I had my days free to explore. That was the deal.

Uncle Stig's belief that I need guidance through the realities of life—the *realpolitik* as he calls it—perfectly complements Dad's grassroots fear of letting me go anywhere or do anything. Between them, they'd crush the life out of me if it weren't for the spirit of Mom fighting back. My memories of her are vague, as she died when I was eight, but her influence is huge. I often imagine how she would have reacted, were she alive today. She was a talented artist who didn't need lofty connections. Although all her paintings were sold to an anonymous buyer and I never got to see her work, her artist spirit guides me through the hardest of times, giving me strength.

Mom abandoned her dreams to be with Dad. Don't get me wrong—Dad's the kindest, most self-sacrificing and downright decent dad a gal could have, but still. She didn't know how long she had left and she spent those years looking after us, facilitating Dad's dreams. Even though her own artistic aspirations lay elsewhere. I can't help but wonder if, given a second chance, she would have done things differently.

And so, I've always done what I can to learn to do stuff for myself so I'll never fall into the trap of depending on a man. It helps that I can read machines pretty well. Change a car tire? Install an oven? Fix a boiler? Check, check, and check. Dad didn't encourage me to learn these things but neither did he discourage me, especially when it became clear

I'd inherited his engineering mindset.

BZZZ! Twenty–four.

And … ignoring.

Uncle Stig pats his pockets. "Is that your phone?"

"Just the alarm."

"This guy, for instance." He pokes his finger at a brochure featuring a local sculptor. "Zero talent. The only reason he has an exhibition is because his mother's close with the Minister of State for Schools."

"Mm–hm."

He flashes me a sympathetic smile. "Don't worry, my dear. You'll be back here again in London pretty soon. I'll make it up to you. Your father can't cling to you forever, especially now that you're an adult."

"I see this trip as the first stepping stone," I say breezily to cover my irritation at his usual dismissal of Dad. "And I really do appreciate all you've done, Uncle Stig."

"We just need to set you up on a new tour, get to know the movers and shakers."

I let him ramble on as we enter the exhibition and wander around the abstract copper and iron sculptures. My mind's made up. I'll never come back here with him. I'll wait until I graduate and have an independent income source—in a few years—and then I'll return on my own terms. No Uncle Stig. No VIP nightclubs.

Maybe he's fulfilling some paternalistic fantasies with me. His own two children are in their early thirties, both engineers, and there's not much he can do to steer them any longer. I probably sent the wrong signals by accepting this trip. I don't need my uncle's help. Any success I will have as an artist will be by merit alone. My teachers are encouraging enough to make me believe it's possible with some really hard work and dedication. And, given my YouTube infamy, it may also involve a name change.

He runs his gaze critically over the uninspired lumps of metal. I'm glad it's keeping his mind off whatever's really bothering him, because something is.

After perusing two levels of twisted metal shapes, we're back at the main entrance. Uncle Stig glances at his watch for the hundredth time. "Nine ten already? I must leave you here, my dear. I hope that's okay with you?"

I try not to let my relief show. He pats me on the shoulder and slinks out the door and disappears into the jostling London commuter crowd.

The Tate's café opens earlier than the museum, so I reckon it's time for a coffee and I'll be first in line for the tickets.

The café inside the Tate is all glass and chrome, uber–cool with a jaw–dropping view of the city. I take a seat by the window overlooking the Thames and finger the delicate vase with a single fresh rose in the center of the table. Since it's early and the café is nearly empty, I've got the best seat.

As I'm mentally tracing the outline of St. Paul's dome, the waitress comes over. "Yes, ma'am?"

"I'll have a cup of coffee and scones with jam and cream, please." I couldn't eat yesterday, so I'm already relishing the powdery dusting of flour on the scones and the sweet fluffy dough inside, peppered with raisins, the thick clotted cream, and most of all the piping hot coffee, which I can already smell.

"Um—?" Her forehead wrinkles. "Aren't you the—aren't you the girl ... the girl from the video? Yes, you are! The duke's wet T–shirt girl!"

The last bit comes out as a screech and all the staff in the café turn in our direction.

Geez, does every Londoner do nothing but watch YouTube? What were the chances? I debate lying, but what would be the point? I'm even wearing the same blazer as last night. I cast my eyes downward.

"Yes."

"Oh my God, c'mere, Janice."

A waitress rushes up. "Lord, it *is* her. I thought so when she walked in. I even said it to Carlos and all."

I purse my lips into a tight smile as she beckons Carlos

over. These people clearly need to get a life.

"So what's he like?" the first waitress asks.

"Did you get a ride in his helicopter?"

"Um, no," I say.

"Oh, here, could I get your autograph?" The waitress called Janice turns around her notepad and shoves it under my nose, followed by a pen.

"Just in case," the first waitress says.

"Yeah, just in case," Janice echoes, with a giggle.

"Just in case what?" I look up into her eager face.

Her eyes widen at my question. "In case you become a duchess."

"Right." I finish my name scrawl—nothing like my usual signature—and hand it back to her. As the café staff mill around, it's clear that I'm not going to have a moment's peace if I stay here.

"I'm sorry." I clutch my purse. "But I have to go. Cancel my order."

I stumble out of the café, back into the main hall, which has become busier and offers some degree of anonymity. It's then that I feel my damn phone buzzing against my hip bone again. I whip it out of my pocket. He's getting to be really annoying. I've stored his contact as "Big Cucumber." I even found a still life image of a cucumber by Pavel Shmarov to add to his profile.

I'm not going to answer. It's either some kind of cat and mouse game for his entertainment, or he really does expect me to pay his dry–cleaning bill. But what if he's tracking the phone? If he is somehow related to the Windsors, then I bet he has access to the highest levels of security and has the power to locate me if he really wants to.

I picture him, lounging on a rococo armchair, following my SIM card's progress through London on a large screen with a little flashing green light to indicate my position, barking out orders to his SWAT team to intercept me. Yes, I'm being paranoid, but Uncle Stig's told me tales of what really goes on behind the scenes in his own embassy, and in a duke's castle, it's probably a level or two more bizarre.

I glance around. At the corner to the left of the gallery entrance, there's a man standing holding the *Financial Times* in front of him like a movie cliché. I'm pretty sure he wasn't there a minute ago. Am I being followed?

The phone feels hot in my hand. It buzzes again. I've lost count now. I'd take the SIM card out, only this freaking phone is impossible to open up without a paperclip and who the hell goes around London carrying a paperclip? A thought strikes me, and I laugh. This phone is an old thing I brought over with me for emergencies. I don't actually need it, especially if I'm flying back tomorrow. When I gaze through the gallery entrance again, the Golden Jubilee footbridges seem to be calling out to me.

I start walking. When I reach the middle of the footbridge, I wait until no other pedestrians are looking, take the phone, and toss it over the railing. Down, down, down it falls into the green–gray murkiness of the Thames. I see a distant splash. A couple of gulls flutter away.

*Ta–dah.* Track that, cocky duke.

How easy was that? One fewer man in my life who's trying to control me. I skip along the bridge feeling lighter, reckless, flushed in victory. No one, not even Dad or Uncle Stig, can reach me now. I have the rest of the day to structure as I want to. I just have to buy a cheap hat and sunglasses so nobody else recognizes me.

# 4

ALEX

She's not answering? *Fuck* this.

We went to a fair amount of trouble on her behalf. Marty confirmed the number was real—temporary SIM purchased on May 16th, two days ago, at Heathrow—and he blocked it from his colleagues. I don't know how many times I called her. Twenty? Fifty? Hell of a lot more than she deserves. I know she's using the phone, because it was engaged one time, so she's decided to ignore me. She's probably packing for her flight tomorrow.

At this stage I just want to wash my hands of Stig Lawson and his fiery little niece. But her hazel eyes keep flashing into my mind and then the image of some scary Azerbaijanis with sawn–off shotguns.

Marty's right—she's nothing like the women I usually bump into at *Jayvees*—the sleek, semi–starving, smooth–talking social butterflies who have my net worth calculated down to the nearest pound sterling. It's her innocence—or perhaps her fake innocence—wrapped up in a smart, sassy–mouthed package that gets to me, I suppose. Her eyes sparkle with an optimism that's hard to find in my jaded circles of entitled women. And her glorious and very natural tits, God help me. Why is that breed of woman so hard to find these days?

I hear squabbling in the next door office. I shove my phone back in my pocket, push my chair away from the desk and get up.

"Tell him, Alex!" Letty says the minute I cross the threshold. My sister flounces her hair back over her shoulders and scowls at Ken sitting opposite her at the conference table strewn with *Town & Country* magazines.

"Tell him what?" I ask.

"If we allow *Town & Country* to feature us in August's edition, it'll help with your Saudi wedding bid."

I smile. Letty's taking my new venture seriously. I know it's a distraction from business as usual—the running of the family eco–farm conglomerate—but I'm hopeless at figuring out the tenants' accounts and Seb certainly didn't make it easy by just disappearing without a trace with no contingency plan. I've got more chance if I start something new.

"I don't see how," Ken says, drumming his fingers on the table. "Abbeydale has ninety–six rooms in much better nick than ours, breath–taking gardens, two hundred thousand visitors last year. The direct comparison can only hurt us."

"We should pull out all the stops for the photoshoot anyway," I say. "Adjust the central heating for the rooms they'll be using, and take off the dust sheets. When is it, Letty?"

"Friday fortnight. Publication in July's edition."

"Okay, we'll call up all the temp staff to come in, get the place shining, and hover impressively in the background on the day."

Ken folds his arms. "Which is a bank holiday, in case you hadn't noticed."

"We'll pay them double."

"Throw more money around, and why not?" he mutters.

"Go sell a racehorse," I retort.

"And you a helicopter," he snaps back.

"I have a piano I could sell." Letty's voice cuts in sweetly.

There's a silence. I can't help but wonder why we've had

some kind of argument like this every single day since Seb disappeared. It all seemed so harmonious before. Part of the reason, of course, is that Ken fears that the Saudi wedding bid will be a flop because it's my idea.

Letty pipes up again. "The Abbeydales aren't nearly as photogenic as we are. Lady Bromwell's hitting fifty. Botox isn't doing it for her. And His Lordship's like a corpse dressed up. I bet the Saudi prince prefers young aristocracy, especially good–looking ones like us."

"And when push comes to shove, he's only a viscount."

Letty and Ken exchange glances.

"It matters," I insist.

"That's not what you said a month ago." Ken leans back in his seat. "If I recall, you said 'fuck the title' as you threatened to throw the coronet in the duck pond."

"Then," Letty adds, "you proposed faking your own death so Ken could become duke."

"You got me on a bad day." It was three days after the funeral and I was still drunk. "Let's focus on now. And I still say we have every chance of snatching this wedding from under old Bromwell's nose."

Letty smacks her lips pensively. "Although with Seb gone, we may have lost some of our star quality."

"Abbeydale's south roof isn't falling in either, is it?" Ken asks.

I sit down beside Letty. "We'll get the roof fixed."

"How?" His brow crinkles up into its familiar withering expression. "It's half an acre of slate. That gobbles up our budget for the rest of the year, especially if you're going to keep cancelling our open days."

"Ken." Letty lets out a dramatic sigh. "You're focusing on the negative. The small details."

"You're an airhead who wouldn't know a detail if it bit you on your surgically–corrected nose."

"All right, all right." I hold up my hand for a ceasefire. "You *are* a tad intense these days, Ken, always sweating the small stuff. Look, we couldn't have open days in a period of mourning."

Ken rises. "And you just walk in with the solution to everything, except you're the biggest problem. Those YouTube videos? I can't see many Saudi princes queueing up to get married here now, can you?"

I glare at him. "He won't care about that. The guy runs a personal harem. I'm a Catholic schoolboy compared to him."

Ken snorts. "Better be right about that."

"Of course I am. Have a little faith. We just need to talk to these people the way they like to be talked to. Why do you think I'm learning Arabic?"

"Yeah, I forgot, good luck with that."

"I think it's brilliant," Letty enthuses.

I flash her a grin. "Thanks, Letty."

There's a long silence.

"If we're talking to a prince, then I should at least have a courtesy title too," Ken grumbles. "He won't know if it's real or not."

"Yes, Alex, you've surely plenty enough to go around— Earl of Cessford, Viscount of Bowmount?" Letty says with a laugh. "Marquess of Tullibardine?"

"Okay, I hereby declare you Viscount of Bowmount," I say in mock solemnity to Ken, happily breaking a venerable 800–year tradition of succession laws.

His face lightens up, which is what I was aiming for. "I want to be Earl."

I pretend to ponder the issue. "Shouldn't we leave that for Seb?"

"All right," he concedes. "Viscount it is."

"What–what?" Letty rises and struts toward me swinging her feather boa under my chin. "Am I to remain empty handed?"

"Countess would suit you." I grin up at her. "But you'd have to marry Peter for that, wouldn't you?"

"Oooh." Her eyes glow with mischief. "He's not the only Earl in Britain, you know."

Although we all end up laughing, my stomach is churning

as it always is at the start of the working day. No incumbent duke wants to be the one who doesn't pass the family estate and business on in a better condition than they received it in. I don't want to be that guy.

But I'm not Seb. I never will be. I don't have his skills, his workaholic temperament, or his magnetic melancholy that seems to make farmers trust him and the rich want to empty their pockets to him.

I was *this* close to hiring a new operations director to sort out the eco–farming business, but Mother begged me not to. She said it would send a signal to Seb that he's not wanted back. That's probably what he's waiting for ... confirmation that the world really is the dark, unwelcoming place he thinks it is. Sheesh.

Meanwhile, I'm left in limbo, not knowing if or when he's coming back from wherever–the–fuck he is. I can keep this game up for another month more, but that's it. If he's not back by then, I'm hiring someone as capable as he is for the tasks of managing this whole shebang, no matter what Mother says. I may have to emigrate if the fallout is too devastating. God knows I wouldn't be the first idle, absentee duke this country has ever known.

But first things first—get ahold of this Hayley person. I can't have her on my conscience, too. I'll try her phone one last time.

Huh. It's not even ringing now. What does that mean? I guess the phone's dead. She probably poured a Cosmopolitan over it. Damn it anyway. I don't know why, but I want to know where she is.

# 5

HAYLEY

"Damn fine looking man, I'll give you that." Mara's red hair bounces in the Skype window as she nods her appreciation. Her excited voice echoes off the hard, polished surfaces of the room as if my bestie's right here with me. I'm upstairs in Winfield House—the ambassadorial residence—in the second drawing room with the eighteenth–century French *boiseries*, marble chimneypiece, and somewhat uncomfortable sofas. I'm waiting for Uncle Stig to be ready so we can leave for Heathrow.

Mara wants to dissect the YouTube video again because it wasn't embarrassing enough the first time around. The hit count is hitting half a million. Every time I watch it, my nipples seem to jut out further. It's a pity they didn't disable the comments because there's a horrendous number of haters out there, keyboard warriors who feel entitled to attack every aspect of my personality and my body. Or maybe that was the whole point.

"Oh yes," I groan. "Big Cucumber improves each time I watch it, whereas I slide closer to slut hell."

Mara giggles. "You sure about the big part? There's not much visible on the video."

"Oh, I'm sure. You can't be that cocky if you're not well

29

endowed—in every sense of the word."

"And you're absolutely sure it was him who kept calling?"

"Unless it was you, Mara, playing a prank, yes."

Her chocolate brown eyes brim with mischief. "I'd have picked up. Just saying."

"Well, it doesn't matter now," I say. Leaving London feels like defeat even after cramming in the Portraits and Tate into a migraine–inducing art marathon yesterday. Mara is about the only person in the world I can bear talking to anymore. She's the only friend who understands the Bermuda Triangle that is the relationship between me, Dad and Uncle Stig. She knows what it meant for me to break free and go on this trip in the first place, and hence she also understands how disappointing this bitter end is.

"How are things over there?" I ask, keen to change the subject. "Any interesting projects come in?"

"Not yet. Still waiting." Her voice is far too perky for an architect's assistant who's done a twelve–hour stint of monkey work. Anyone else would be wilting away if they worked as she did—interning for Mike's little architectural office while studying in Portland at the same time. I suspect I'm the first person she's talked to today apart from her slave-driver.

"Oh, I met your dad at lunchtime in Freddy's and he didn't mention YouTube, so you're safe for the moment. He's so isolated, Hayley. This is the one time you should appreciate your rustic existence out on the gorge."

Okay, so she's talked to Dad. She often does because he's so much nicer to her than her own emotionally retarded father. "Yeah, but the flight's fifteen hours," I say gloomily. "That's a long time on the Internet."

"Should I go over and guard your house and protect him from any gossipy neighbors?"

"Would you?" I ask, knowing it's impossible.

Mara shakes her head in amusement. "What did you tell him about your phone anyway?"

I shrug. "That I lost it." That particular email went out a

few minutes ago. No details. I hate lying, especially to Dad. "Oh, Mara, I'm dreading landing this evening. He'll be so disappointed. This is exactly the kind of thing he was worried about."

"No, he was worried about you getting abducted, not flashing your tits at a duke." Mara's struggling not to laugh. "Although I don't know how thrilled he'll be when he does see it."

I bury my head in my hands. "It's practically porn."

"All you can do is pretend it's a stunt to draw attention to your ... body of work."

"Uncle Stig's saying the same thing."

"Well, he seems to know a lot about infamy. I'd say his days are numbered as ambassador."

I lift my head up again. "No, Mara, Uncle Stig's innocent. It's that stupid duke trying to frame him for something, just for kicks. It's a setup of some kind. The question is why? Surely he's got a whole cabinet of British ministers he could trash if he wanted to—"

There's a knock on the door.

I leap up. "Hold on a sec, someone at the door. Back in a sec."

It's my uncle, all dressed for outside with his navy Burberry overcoat and matching scarf and umbrella. He strides in, wringing his hands. His gaze darts around the room. "Who were you talking to?"

"Just Mara." I point to my Skype window.

"Right. Hayley, I'm afraid we need to change plans again. The flights, we can't get them. I'm told it's not safe."

"What?"

Uncle Stig strides in a circle, throttling his umbrella, so agitated he's unaware how ridiculous he looks. I'm pretty sure I look stupid too with my mouth hanging open in sheer disbelief. Not being able to take a flight sounds serious. Who or what could prevent us from exercising our rights to travel as US citizens? We're so diplomatically immune he could murder someone and then hop on the next plane first–class

31

SARA FORBES

and demand a gin martini.

When he's done four circles of the Persian rug, I ask, "What's going on?"

He flaps his hand at my laptop to indicate I should close it.

I mouth "bye" to Mara whose expression is as aghast as mine. I shut the lid.

Uncle Stig's fervent eyes beam from his craggy face. "You see, my dear, in my position ... there sometimes comes a time when we have to compromise on certain matters in order for the wheels of diplomacy to turn at all. Do you understand what I'm saying?"

I nod. I've listened to enough of his conversations to appreciate the sentiment, the idea that politics can be murky and subjective at times. But how would that stop us taking our flight home?

"I made a mistake with certain people. It's something I must correct while I'm here."

I'm so flabbergasted my uncle's admitting to making a mistake that I just give a cautious, "O–kay."

"Good." He leans on the umbrella like it's a walking stick. "Good. Good. So, let's check out from the hotel and head anywhere but Heathrow."

"But where?"

When he doesn't answer, I say, "Come on, I need to tell Dad something, or he'll call Winfield house, or the embassy, or even the police when he doesn't hear from me. You know he will."

"Don't call him ... not yet." Uncle Stig's voice thickens. "Look, Hayley, it would just upset him. Your dad never had an understanding for ... nuance. You on the other hand, you're a smart girl."

I bristle at the insinuation that Dad's not smart. Dad may be quiet and modest, but at least he'd never get caught scrapping with the British aristocracy on YouTube.

My uncle sits down heavily in the armchair opposite. "I have ties with Azerbaijani businessmen who were expecting a

32

diplomatic favor from me, one I chose not to follow through on. It wasn't the right time. So now, I need to lay low, and so do you. Because after that YouTube affair, they know you're here. These Azerbaijani businessmen are unhappy. I can't risk them threatening us in any way. Do you understand what I'm saying?"

A cold wave of fear washes over me. Is someone *threatening* him? *Us?* It's swiftly followed by anger. Because of that goddamn duke? I don't even begin to understand it, so I focus on practicalities. "How'm I supposed to lay low, Uncle Stig? The whole of Britain seems to know my face."

He comes over and engulfs me in a hug that I'm not expecting. He has his warm moments, I suppose, even if they intrude at unexpected times. "It'll be fine. I'm working on it. There's nothing for you to worry about. Now grab your bags, and let's go. There's a private car waiting outside."

"But where are we going?" I cry.

"We'll … see."

This isn't the answer I want to hear.

This is freaking *unbelievable.* We're in the back of an Audi A6, crawling at snail's pace through the London morning traffic. I stare out the blackened windows at the billboards of advertisements jarring against the grim aesthetics of an east London residential street. Drizzle spatters against the glass.

Just forty–eight hours ago, I'd been so excited to be here. It was a new beginning. Now, my life's in danger and I don't know where I'll be sleeping tonight and Uncle won't tell me what the hell is really going on.

"Can't we just stay in Winfield House or go to the embassy?" I ask.

"No," comes my uncle's swift response. "On both counts. The man I was contacted by—an officer in MI6—he arranged this car, this driver,"—Uncle Stig beckons to the thick–necked driver in sunglasses, who doesn't even flinch—

"and told me in no uncertain terms to hide somewhere unofficial until I hear back from him."

I slump back against the leather upholstery and watch Uncle Stig out of the side of my eyes. He's busy dialing up people from a list of paper balancing on his knee with thirty–odd numbers scrawled on it. There's a pattern. He'll get past the pleasantries, which can take anything from two minutes to quarter of an hour, depending on how much they're into golf, then he'll mumble something about it being a long time since they'd met. The conversations die abruptly after that. I wonder whether he's purposely contacting his list of flaky friends or these are the only kind he has. Surely the US ambassador has been able to foster better quality friendships than this in his adopted country?

When he sinks his forehead into his hand, I know the news can't be good.

"End of the list?" I venture.

He looks up with weary eyes. "Yeah."

We stare out our respective windows. We've reached the M25 and it's as congested with traffic as all the legends would have it, but at least it's moving now that the morning rush is over.

"Is there nobody?" I ask. "Nowhere?"

"I need somewhere private." He grips his phone as if to punish it for the flakiness of his so–called friends. "Civilian, non–government, impartial." He sighs. "Isolated."

I don't know if it's because we're passing a Cartier ad, but a thought strikes me at that precise moment. "The duke," I murmur. "He got us into this trouble, least he could do is suggest a good hiding place."

Uncle Stig lowers his phone to his lap. For a moment, he's speechless. Then he says, "That's actually *perfect.*"

"Uh, what?"

His eyes widen in delight. "The *Duke* … that's the perfect cover. No one would ever suspect we'd be with him."

"Be with him?" I repeat in horror.

"Do you have his number?" he asks.

I nod, dumbly.

"Call him."

"I … lost my phone."

He starts googling.

"It's okay, Uncle Stig." I let out a harried breath. "I know his number."

My uncle thrusts his phone into my hand. "Then call him."

I'm glad he doesn't ask how I know the stupid number. I ignored it so often yesterday I know it off by heart. And something tells me we'll have more luck calling that number than my uncle's had with his dozens of useless acquaintances. I'd prefer Uncle Stig screamed that he wanted nothing to do with that cocky, entitled bastard—but no, it appears he is actually serious.

As my index finger hesitates over the green icon, he says, "Hayley, we don't have much choice. You have to try." His tone is unrelenting. I've heard it so often in his arguments with Dad. It's best to give in early than have my will broken down in painful stages, as so often happens to Dad.

As I hold the ringing phone to my ear, my stomach churns, a mix of bile and the dry croissant I stuffed down my throat just before the call with Mara earlier. Best to get it over with. If the duke says no, which in all likelihood he will, then I'll never have to speak to him again.

But what if he says yes?

# 6

ALEX

I'm tucking into my pudding—pears from the estate orchard steeped in red wine with thick cream—when my phone buzzes against my hip. I slide it out under the hem of the tablecloth. No caller ID. Ugh.

I excuse myself, leave the lunch table, and collapse into the chair in the Blue Room, three doors down. It's still ringing. They're persistent, I'll give them that.

"Fernborough, Belgrave Castle," I say in my most bored tone.

"Oh," comes a surprised, female voice.

I know that voice. Happiness floods my system and my dick comes alive. I suddenly realize why I've been so out of sorts the past two days.

There's a pause, like she didn't expect me to answer my own phone. Judging by the background noise, she's in a car or something. Her breathless voice comes again. "So ... it's ... it's you. I mean, of course it is. Um ... well. I–I'm sorry about the ... the you know. I saw the YouTube video and I didn't know—I didn't know—"

She seems incapable of stringing a coherent sentence together, but then again, I often have that effect on women. With her voice, the memory of the rest of Hayley Cochrane comes back in a flash. Bits I'd forgotten that the video didn't catch—her luscious lips revealing her pearly whites as she speaks, the way her eyes seem to shine with good–natured optimism.

"You didn't know how important I was?" I finish for her, idly twisting the gold tassels on a lampshade.

"Well, no."

Another pause follows, where I imagine she's biting her plump bottom lip, wondering what to say next, wondering how to appease me. I let the pause drag out this time as I gaze around at the light blue silk wallpaper that gave this room its name, at the Reynolds, the Canaletto, the Sargent—paintings I rarely stop to look at. I wish I could watch her squirm in person. Yes, I could summon her here, to Belgrave Castle, and order her to stand in front of me and beg for what she wants. First I'd pretend to be angry and make her beg for forgiveness—

"I need your help." Her voice is tight, scared almost. I sit up straighter. Of course she needs my help with an uncle such as that.

"What can I do for you?" I say. Her anxious tone is threatening to interrupt my fantasy whereby she's now kneeling in front of me and begging. Naked. Mm–mm. I'm getting hot under the collar now. I loosen my tie.

"I'm in trouble. My uncle's in trouble. We need a safe place to hide. Just for a short while."

There are tears in her voice. I've been witness to too many tearful women not to recognize the signs even over a phone line. It even sounds genuine. I'd like to say my heart is touched by her plight, but the only organ reacting to any of this is much further south.

"And how may I help with that?"

She sighs but sounds irritated now. I don't want her to cut me off, so I smoothly add, "Unless of course you're thinking of paying me a little visit here in Belgrave Castle?"

There's a kind of muffled sigh from her end.

"Our family estate," I continue. "Just down the road from

Fernborough on the A336. It's a safe haven. You'd be in excellent company. We've been hiding all kinds of renegades here over the centuries, most notably Brendan of St. Downes in 1765, pretender to the throne. Eventually they chopped his head off, but that was only after he left our hospitality."

"Well, that's real nice, Mister ... um, Duke."

"Alex, to you."

"Alex," she repeats in a careful voice and the way her gentle, US West Coast accent caresses the name gets my mind spinning in all directions. I want to hear her scream it out. In brainless ecstasy. Again and again. As I bend her over the nearest table, those Hello Kitty panties down by her ankles. My dick is straining against my suit trousers now.

"Say that again," I say.

"What?"

"My name."

There's a pause now. Long enough to tell me she's not playing this game with me. Or maybe she is playing. In any case, all I hear from her side is something between a sniff and a sigh and the background noise of vehicles rumbling and horns beeping. Okay, okay, so she's in trouble. I need to focus. "Why me? Surely I'm the last person your uncle wants to see right now?"

"That's why," she says. "Nobody'll suspect it."

She has a point there. Smart girl. "All right." I'm not too keen on having him under my roof, reinforcing any would–be conspiracy theories about me being involved in his messy dealings, but I'm definitely warming up to the idea of having his luscious, little niece here. "I'll help you."

I hear her sharp intake of breath. "You will?"

"Yes, even if you ignored my call a hundred times yesterday."

"Twenty–six," she corrects.

I like how certain she sounds.

"You didn't answer. What's different now?"

"I didn't know, Alex. I didn't know ... what Uncle Stig was caught up in." Her voice is meek and confused. I preferred it when she was being snarky. Last thing I need is another tearful woman on the phone, especially if I didn't have the pleasure of a night before to compensate for it.

"It's a right mess, that's what it is," I say. "Serve him right, too."

"Well, that's hardly fair."

"He's there, isn't he?" I ask.

"Yes."

"Whereabouts are you?"

"Heading onto the M25, at Junction 29 … uh, there's a sign, wait a minute, it's a place called Codham Hall Wood."

"Perfect, turn off at Junction 28, and head into Brentwood village. I'll send a car. The driver is George Seymour. He'll pick you up outside the cathedral in a silver Bentley. Don't get in unless he confirms this name."

"Okay, got it. I don't know how to thank you."

I can barely contain my smirk. "I'm sure you'll think of something."

7

HAYLEY
I feel like I've entered some kind of alternate reality.

My feet crunch on the pale gravel underfoot as we make our way up to the main steps of Belgrave Castle, the duke's ancestral home. Even the gravel looks designer made. Yes, I'm focusing on the minutiae of my surroundings—a defense mechanism to prevent my head from bursting with the craziness of this situation. I refuse to let the majestic surroundings intimidate me. Money means nothing to me. And yet, when I got my first glimpse of the castle, I can't deny having a bit of an Elizabeth Bennet moment where she spots Pemberley for the first time. I mean, Winfield House is pretty impressive, but this is four times the size.

My head has been spinning ever since a frail–looking man in a peaked, mustard cap calling himself George Seymour intercepted Uncle Stig and me outside Brentwood Cathedral. My uncle sent our own driver away and we jumped into the back of the silver Bentley without a murmur of a question, too nerve–wracked to protest at anything. I can only be thankful the duke wasn't sitting in the car waiting for us.

After a silent two-hour drive, George leaves us at the entrance to a large square courtyard as vehicles can't go any further, and instructs us to take the middle path through the rose garden. Uncle Stig is telling me to keep my head up. I fantasize about dunking his head into the duck pond over there. It's all his fault we're in this mess and yet he only had a spectator's part in the groveling session I endured in the car with His Grace Alex fucking Belgrave, 13th Duke of fucking Fernborough. I may not be the world's most experienced woman, but I can tell when a guy is gearing up for some action or whatever quaint euphemism he might have for sex. It's not going to happen.

It's not that I don't find him attractive—of course I do. Anyone would. It's just that his looks, his title, his endowment are all irrelevant to me. I'm not impressed by inherited wealth. I'm studying hard for the highest grade possible so I can lead an authentic life where I've earned all my rewards. I can't imagine living life on any other terms. My glimpse into my uncle's world has told me enough. I don't even want to *know* how the one percent lives.

I lift my head higher as we approach the castle entrance. The garden is truly breathtaking, and May is the month when I suspect it really shines. It must need an army of gardeners all year round to keep it looking like this. Dad would give his right foot to fish in a lake like that. Mara would go wild over the architecture. I need to remember to take lots of photos when nobody's looking.

It screams old money. Of course. I've only seen gardens and castles like this in books and period dramas. I'm sure my manners and my accent will stick out a mile here. My suitcase of clothes is less "lady of the manor" and more "hipster chic" and that's being generous. If I'm expected to swan around in la–di–da dresses, I swear I'm going to find a secret passage to crawl into and hide until the coast is clear.

On that thought, I look up to see the tall, dark–haired man standing at the entrance to the castle, or should I say *posing*. Alex is at the top of the stairs with a navy blazer draped over his forearm, his hand slapped against a stone monument—a lion's head whose snarl has weathered into amiability. In a luminously white shirt, a gold, silk cravat loosened around his collar and top buttons undone, I must say he's looking very *ducal* in his natural habitat.

We move nearer. The sunlight gleams off his dark hair, threading it with copper lines. Wisps of his fringe break the plane of his forehead. His wolf eyes—they're in shadows right now—I imagine are targeted on me. His grin is smug, his generous lips tilted up slightly to one side. My gaze trails further down his body which tapers in at the waist, accentuated by a gold buckle in an interesting coat of arms design. He's wearing impeccable black trousers which lead down lean legs into polished, leather shoes.

Yep, he's hotter than ever.

Uncle Stig and I halt at the bottom of the steps. For a moment, there's an awkward silence and nobody moves. All we hear is the twittering of birds in the bushes and the breeze in the trees. Then Alex moves, stepping quickly down the steps and meeting us halfway with a hand outstretched toward my uncle.

"Ambassador," he says, and they shake.

"Your Grace," Uncle Stig replies, and I want to throttle him for sounding like a goddamned butler.

The duke cocks his head toward me. "Hayley. Please, come up, come up." His voice is all warmth, more so than I remember from Jayvee's. We could be long–lost friends the way he's saying this. He's a good actor.

As we ascend the steps, I'm feeling off–kilter. My uncle seems to be adopting some kind of wait–and–see policy because for once he hasn't theorized on how this is going to all pan out.

We reach the top and stand in front of the duke. I'm made aware that I'm biting down on my bottom lip by the way he's focusing on it, so I stop doing that and raise my chin higher. "We appreciate your help, Duke ... Alex."

"Just Alex, please. I trust your journey was comfortable?" he asks smoothly, looking at Uncle Stig.

My uncle uses the smile he reserves for TV reporters. "Indeed, Your Grace."

I've got to hand it to them. For two men who were at each other's throats the other day, they're embracing the genteel act pretty convincingly.

"I trust your mother is well?" Uncle Stig adds.

A pensive look traverses Alex's face. "As well as can be expected, thank you." His grin appears again. "Please, let's get inside. My man George will take your luggage in."

We trail after him, our footsteps echoing in the massive hall. My eyes devour the details greedily, my gaze landing on a perfect, gilded Louis XIII table. Can that really be a genuine piece? I step toward it and run my fingers along the bumps of the ornate edge, the way you're never allowed do in museums.

Alex slides up beside me. I feel his presence behind my back. I remember how his fingers felt on my neck in Jayvee's and my hairs stand on end again.

"You like it?" He catches my eye in the mirror that hangs over it.

I whip my hand away. "It's exquisite. Is it genuine?"

"As far as I've been told."

"Wow." I can't resist gliding my fingers over the polished surface, as others must have done down the centuries.

"Touch all you like," he says. His gaze is unwavering in the antique mirror, and I can't hold it for long. My face starts to burn. Swiftly, he turns and walks over to Uncle Stig. Inexplicably, my body wants him back beside me. My mind wants him talking to me like this.

*Touch all you like.*

Yeah, right.

When I glance over, my uncle's got a half smile on his face as he eyeballs Alex and me.

I roll my eyes and go over. I don't want anything being decided behind my back. I refuse to be a pawn in this game. Since I got off the plane two days ago, I haven't taken a solitary step in this country that hasn't been somehow dictated by some man or another. I should be trying to find a plan B, but without money to spare, the options are few. Maybe hitchhike to the Scottish Highlands?

"... delicate situation," Uncle Stig's saying in a hushed tone. "But I'm grateful for your help." He sounds like a contrite offender. It gets on my nerves. The magnanimous look Alex gives him in return only makes matters worse.

The tension of the past twenty–four hours has twisted my body into knots of agitation. I'm ready to explode. I've never been good at holding my temper, or counting to ten, or any of that shit.

"Look, this is all your fault." My raised voice echoes in the cavernous hall and I lower it slightly. "If you hadn't messed with my uncle's business, he could have done what he needed to and I'd still be touring galleries."

Alex turns to me with an unreadable expression in his glittering eyes. "If you hadn't chucked your phone in the Thames, I could've told you *yesterday* how much shit you're in."

I turn to Uncle Stig and he just nods.

"How do you know about that?" I fume.

His bright blue eyes drill into me. "Sources."

So, I was being followed. I knew it. That guy with the newspaper. Creepy. It's like Alex is showing off, making it clear who the alpha dog is when it comes to being ahead of the law. And frankly, I'm disappointed with my uncle getting himself into a position where he has to kowtow to this guy. "I suppose you've got the whole of Her Majesty's secret service wrapped around your finger?"

"Hayley, please." Uncle Stig takes a pained breath.

"Okay, okay." I prod my fingers against my forehead. "Is there—like, a bathroom or a bedroom or somewhere where I can just go and be alone for a while? I think I've got a headache coming on."

Like a chameleon, he's back to all lord of the manor courtesy then. "I'm so sorry. I'm being unforgivably negligent. Mrs. Bershley—we just call her Mrs. B—she'll look after you. I'll call for her. Please, come with me."

I'm unable to say anything because Alex's hand is on the small of my back guiding me along, gentle, but insistent.

Much as I hate to say it, it's the first thing that feels good today.

# 8

ALEX

It's half past four and it's time to check on my guests. I've given them two hours to get settled in their rooms with the help of the ever–capable Mrs. Bershley. Back in the south tower—a separate building holding our business offices— Ken and Letty are negotiating the final wording of our Saudi wedding bid, which is, of course, where I should be, but the temptation to bunk off work is just too much.

It's nice and quiet in the main house. Mother's out to afternoon tea with Lady Penrith–Jones. I haven't figured out how I'm going to explain to everyone the presence in our home of a disgraced US ambassador and a YouTube starlet. They've all seen the videos. As of yet, nobody but the staff knows they're here. I could pass it off as a diplomatic courtesy but everyone in my family knows what I think of Stig Lawson. The most plausible excuse for having them here and forbidding my family to speak of it is the media uproar I've caused. I'll pretend to feel guilty.

Marty says I have to keep them here for at least a week. Because, as he put it, a week is a long time in dirty politics. By then, the Azerbaijani oil barons will enter some alternate agreement with Lawson, or his lawyers will find some way to threaten them back. Boom. Done. Marty claims that this kind of thing happens all the time with diplomats. I told him I didn't want to know.

I'm appalled that such a man can become ambassador, and from such a family. His father was nothing short of a criminal the way he built up his newspaper empire. His sister, Hayley's mum, was apparently an artist, but I'd bet my bottom dollar that gallery was just a vehicle for money laundering. They're the kind of people my mother would witheringly call "opportunistic."

I've seen the way the uncle eyes me like a juicy steak whenever I talk to his niece. It's clear he's got some designs on her future here. I wonder if she shares his delusion. There's only one way to find out.

Hayley's bedroom door is closed, so I knock. I told Mrs. Bershley to put the uncle on the third floor, away from Hayley's on the first and mine on the second. I don't want him monitoring who goes in or out of our rooms.

"Come in," she says. So I do.

She bolts upright on the bed as I close the door behind me. Eyes wide, hair a little mussed, cheeks pinker than before.

"Oh I didn't—"

"Expect me?"

*Nice try.* I hide my smirk by strolling to the window. There, I turn, lean my arse against the windowsill and watch how the light falls on her face, her throat, that tremendous *au naturel* rack of hers. She's wearing a baggy T-shirt and trousers. I guess they're her pajamas. There's nothing sexy about them, but the way she fills them out is accidentally erotic.

I shift my weight onto my other foot. Her eyes are following my hands, so I drop them to my belt, hooking my thumbs inside. Of course, I could accelerate the proceedings. Talk a bit, draw her out, get her to laugh, move close, make her feel she's beautiful, make my move, but I want her to come to me, begging. That's the fantasy I started with, so I'm going to see it through. I want her to be wet. I want her eyes to be hungry. I want—

"Alex?" she says and my eyes pop open. What just happened there? Had I closed them?

"Yes, Hayley?"

"Why are you helping me?"

"You asked me to." *Begged. You begged, didn't you?* And while that felt really good on the phone, it's going to be a hundred times better now, in person. As soon as she gets over this disinterested little act of hers. Doesn't she realize I've seen it a hundred times before?

A frown creases her forehead. "But you could have refused."

"It's not my style to refuse a damsel in distress." I attempt a grin, but her voice, it's getting to me. The fact that she's talking at all is getting to me. She should be moaning. She shouldn't be sitting there with her questions and with her tits ready to burst through the fabric, a little gold chain tantalizingly trapped between the two firm mounds of golden, sun–kissed skin. She should be flat on her back offering those beauties to my mouth. I'd know how to look after them.

But no, she's still just sitting there, propped up against the pillows, legs stretched out. Legs I want with all my being to ease apart as I lick my way to their apex.

I leave my place at the window and approach the bed. I stand there, looking down. She should be doing something by now, something to show she's interested, but she's just staring back innocently. My shadow falls across her outstretched legs. She inhales a sharp breath as she continues to look up into my face. I cock my head like a goddamn spaniel but my focus homes in on her nipples, which have oh so gloriously hardened, punching tiny bumps though the fabric.

I allow my gaze to linger on those hardened pebbles, letting her know I know. I look up to see her gaze flickering down to my crotch, as if to say touché. Finally we're getting places. By the time she looks back into my eyes, her cheeks have become infused with a darker shade of pink and her breath is coming faster. I'm sure mine is too. I love this part. The part when she says something coy and breathless and gloriously silly. Bonus points if she then removes some clothing, without my asking her to.

"Excuse me, did you have something to tell me?" Her voice is flat, not a hint of coquetry. Her eyes are glinting with something hard.

"Actually, I wasn't planning on doing a lot of talking."

"Well if you expect me to kneel down and suck your dick to show my gratitude, don't bother, because I'm packing my bags right now."

I back up, hands raised and nearly trip over the rug as I step away from the bed. "Whoa, easy there."

This has never happened before. I tend to go for older, experienced types who are more likely to advance on me. She's what? Twenty? Twenty–one? Not very experienced. She doesn't seem to have even caught on to the fact that she's expected to be paying me some dues here.

I resume my place at the window, watching her. Several deep breaths later, I've calmed down. All right, there's no hurry. I've got time to do this right since she's stuck here for a few days at least, according to Marty. She's not going anywhere, because she's got nowhere to go.

I can teach her stuff she's never experienced with anyone else. Teach her how showing appreciation is meant to be done. I can be the one in control and tease out her pleasure ... slowly, so she's desperate to give me everything she's got. But first I need to train her not to fear me.

"Dinner." I say heading for the door. "Will you be joining us for dinner? It's at six if you feel so inclined. I'll come back then to collect you." I'm fighting to keep frustration out of my voice, but I feel proud, too, at my self–control.

"Dinner?" I hear her say faintly as I go out the door. The scorn in her voice makes me grit my teeth.

That didn't go the way I meant it to.

# 9

HAYLEY
Is a bedroom door key too much to ask, goddammit?

By a quarter to six, I've recovered, somewhat. Alex bursting in on me in my unsexy pajamas wasn't one of the greater moments of my existence. In my defense, minutes before that, I was all good and ready to sink my head into those heavenly goose–down pillows and forget the world. I mean, everybody's touchy when they're half asleep.

I'm feeling perkier after that shower—a gloriously hot jet–spray, way better than in Winfield House. Escaping from Uncle Stig for a few hours has also elevated my mood to the point where I'm ready to take on any bullshit Alex decides to throw at me and fling it right back at him. There was a moment where he looked completely caught off guard—*lost*—and I'm replaying that over and over again. All I need is a little chink in his armor.

After much deliberation on what to wear to a duke's dining table, I've chosen a white top—polyester, but might look like silk by candlelight—a small string of pearls, classy black jeans with no rips, and black pumps. This is the height of sophistication that can be mustered out of the contents of my suitcase.

I dial up Skype. I got the password for the Wi–Fi by

simply asking Mrs. Bershley. I've had plenty of time to concoct a story for Dad. The poor man thinks we cut our trip short because Uncle Stig wanted to attend an urgent meeting and that we're sitting on a plane somewhere over the Atlantic by now.

Dad's face is already wincing up in fatherly concern as I breezily tell him that my uncle has to meet some businessmen and I've been invited by a duke to stay at Belgrave Castle and it would be impolite to refuse so we've decided to change our return flights once again.

"Duke? Who's this duke?" Dad asks in understandable exasperation.

"He's a friend of Uncle Stig's."

"That's not reassuring."

At least this means Dad still hasn't seen my YouTube clip. I'm beginning to wonder just how isolated he keeps himself when I'm not around. He's probably spent most of his time alone out fishing. "It's a beautiful castle and a lovely family who've made me very welcome, and it's a fabulous opportunity to spend a few more days in England experiencing the culture. And the art, Dad. The walls are dripping with it."

He rubs his forehead. "Those are not your kind of people."

Behind him, I see the kitchen looking suspiciously clean, bathed in orange morning sunlight, the wooden surfaces clear, the floor mats positioned at right–angles instead of diagonals which I'd have insisted on. No fresh flowers. A tell–tale stack of empty pizza boxes. He hasn't been eating properly. I get a pang for home. "Come on home now, Hayley."

"Dad, it's not that simple."

"I think it is." Dad's forehead creases into deep grooves of worry. It's weird to talk to him on camera, which seems to amplify the anxiety in his face.

"I'm fine. Really."

"Why wouldn't you be fine?" he asks, suspicion now

trumping concern. It's really hard to lie to Dad.

"Look, I'll ask Uncle Stig to book us for Friday. Give us 'til Friday? Please?" I'm hoping three days is long enough for my uncle to sort out whatever he needs to with those Azerbaijanis. As Dad as always said, he's the kind of guy who could negotiate his way out of hell if it ever came to it.

"Friday," Dad repeats.

I hate lying. I want to comfort him and to reassure him everything's going to be fine, that I'm safe, but am I?

A knock on the door interrupts us. "Dad, sorry, I need to go. I'll call you again later." I click off the camera before he can protest.

I open up. It's Alex. Dashing as ever in a light blue shirt that I'll admit does wondrous things to his eyes.

"Hello." I flash him a small, insincere smile.

His full grin appears. "You look fantastic. Are you guarding the Crown Jewels behind that door by any chance?"

"Not that I know of. Why?"

He knocks on the wood. "You're gripping onto it for dear life."

He's right. *Relax, Hayley.* Even if he is so ... overwhelming, that doesn't mean he's out to take advantage of me. Maybe he does just want to help out of the goodness of his heart. I need to cut him some slack here. Maybe it's normal for them to walk into each other's rooms all the time. It's a family home after all, not a hotel. I hold open the door wider.

He remains in the corridor. "Come on out, sweet girl, I won't bite." He sounds like the wolf talking to Little Red Riding Hood.

"You won't?"

His smile broadens. "Only if you'd like me to."

I laugh. "Let's not ruin your appetite before dinner."

As we saunter down the carpeted corridor, I feel him watching me. My top has a low back but it's otherwise demure. I wonder what he's thinking, so I turn around and his eyes dart back up to my face.

52

"This way." His voice is soft and low in my ear. Goosebumps form all down my arms when he guides me with a caress above my elbow. We're turning left.

"Your uncle's room is up this way," he says as we reach the staircase. Funny, I expected Uncle Stig's room to be nearer to mine. Are they trying to give us the impression that they actually use all the intervening rooms?

On the second stair, his thumb grazes my shoulder blade through the opening in my blouse, as if accidentally. I stiffen and stop moving. Then his entire hand is splayed against my spine, half way down my back. It's a brazen gesture but I do nothing but stare straight ahead at the stairs we're supposed to ascend. Finally, his hand slides down to my lower back leaving a rippling trail of pleasure under my skin. My groin tightens. I'm light headed. I want him to keep doing that.

His voice comes as a low rumble in my ear. "My room's to the right." I follow his pointing finger to the second door on the right.

"O–kay. Good to know."

"Just in case."

I look up into his face, challenging him. His body may have temporarily given me a thrill, yes, but he shouldn't think I'm so weak that I can't question his motives. He's soon going to find out that I can resist him just fine and have my own life, which is every bit as important as his, waiting for me back in Laxby, Oregon. "Just in case what?"

"You get scared." His hand on my spine rotates in a tiny circle, kneading the muscles. It's mind–numbingly pleasurable as his touch gets softer and sexier, like a feather. "We have ghosts and shit."

"I'll bear it in mind," I murmur, biting my lower lip as I continue climbing stairs. His fingers remain on my spine and with every light press of his fingertips into my skin, I want him to move further down, or up, I don't know which. The way he plays me feels so damn good. His hands are nowhere near my front, but my nipples are painfully hard. And something tells me he knows this, that he's been reading women from an early age.

At the landing of the third set of stairs, I clasp the thick banister and take a long, shuddering breath. I'm a mess and he knows it as he stands there cool as, well, a cucumber.

"Okay, let's go get your uncle," he says. His hands fall away from my body. I gasp at the loss but I cover it up with a cough.

## 10

ALEX

As we make our approach to the dining room, it's all I can do not to let Ambassador Lawson wander on ahead so I can corner Hayley in an alcove and begin this thing. Despite her scornful tone, she seems to want it. Well, her body does, even if her brain might need persuasion. We may have some fun after dinner. That is, if my family doesn't tear her to pieces first.

Everyone's there when we enter—Mother, Letty, and Ken. They're sitting primly at the dining table, waiting for the three empty spaces to be filled. Under Mother's instruction, Hayley takes the place on Ken's side, Lawson on Letty's, and I take the head of the table, opposite Mother. Father's old position is usually occupied by Seb and I still don't feel comfortable in it, but Mother insists I sit there to "balance out the table."

Mother straightens her spine and graces Hayley and Lawson with a faint smile. "I'm glad Mrs. B had the presence of mind to tell cook in time that we had guests."

Mrs. B slides me a look that says *you're on your own* and hurries out of the room with a tray of dishes.

The whole table awaits my official explanation of our guests' presences and my absence from work this afternoon, even though it's clear they've all formed their own opinions.

There still needs to be an official explanation, because that's how things are done in my family.

I clear my throat. "Well, I met Hayley in London and we decided to spend some time together for a few days before she flies back to Oregon. After our incident in Jayvee's, which I'm sure you're aware of, I decided it's best she wait it out here until the media circus dies down. Her uncle—Stig, here—just happened to have some time off too, and he's offering his assistance on the Saudi wedding deal. He has great experience with public tenders, which can only help our application."

I take stock of their reactions, daring anyone to question as much as a syllable of it. They don't believe a word of it, but that isn't the point. "Please make them both welcome in our home."

Mother gives a tiny nod. "Surprise guests are always a pleasure." What she means is the total opposite, but it's better than nothing. Besides, she of all people could do with a little distraction. "Welcome to our home, Ambassador Lawson, Hayley."

"It's Stig, please," Lawson clarifies.

Hayley says a quiet, "Thank you." Her stiff posture conveys all the discomfiture I'd expect her to feel in her position. I can't make this any easier for her.

Mother tugs her linen napkin from its ivory ring. It signals that we can all eat now. Nobody says grace anymore. That was Father's thing. Mother seems to believe we've been forsaken and there is nothing to be particularly grateful to any deity for. Me, I'm just praying this meal can finish without some kind of disaster.

Ken shakes his head in silence and starts spooning asparagus soup into his mouth.

Letty beams at our two guests and pours Chardonnay into everyone's crystal goblets. It's a decent vintage. We get it from a small vineyard outside Beaune that we pick up on the drive back from our villa. Then she breaks the silence in her loud, plummy voice. "Well, I think it's *too* thrilling to have some visitors again." With a flick of her hair, she laughs her big laugh. Letty takes life on its own terms and finds it amusing for reasons no one else can quite fathom. It can be irritating at times but right now her laughter is a welcome sound.

Hayley smiles at her.

I give my sister the evil eye so she won't get it into her head to start an interrogation. "How's the Saudi wedding going?" I ask.

"Fine, no thanks to you." Ken points at me with his spoon. "No disrespect to your guests, but if you'd other plans for this afternoon, all you had to do was let us know."

"You seem to have handled it just fine."

"We talked to the head of their wedding council, a man of some importance. They expected the heir to be present. It's an insult otherwise. I told him you'd call him this evening." Ken's eyes glitter with schadenfreude because he knows I had other plans, specifically with the guest sitting to his left.

"Fine," I snap.

Ken slurps his soup with relish. "This wouldn't have happened if you'd just showed up when you were supposed to."

"Alex must've got all tied up," Letty says with a wicked smile.

I know what my sister's thinking. She's seen me in compromising positions—women running out of my bedroom missing garments or fully naked. She's seen a woman bound to the posts of my bed with four Hermes silk scarves. I'm not proud of that moment, but I was only twenty–two and Patty Whatshername did insist on it and even provided the scarves. I'm much better at locking my bedroom door these days.

"Letty, just shut up." I throw a look at Hayley. Her eyes are huge pools of darkness, burning out from the cheeks that are flushed pink. Her lips are slightly parted in shock. The tiny diamond–shaped hole of her mouth draws my attention. I want to fill that delicate parting, ease it wider and wider with my lips, then my tongue.

She's driving me mad with her porcelain, virginal act. Where was all that primness when she leapt over that bar in Jayvee's? When she poured a drink very precisely over my cock? I'm starting to feel cheated.

"Alex?" Letty's pouring water out of a jug.

"Mind you don't spill it on him," Ken says to her.

"Ah, it's only water, not a Cosmopolitan," Letty shoots back and they both burst into laughter.

I glance at Hayley, trying to signal that she should just ignore all this. To my relief, she's got a half smile on her face.

"Do you ride?" Letty asks Hayley.

Hayley's face lights up. "Yes."

Yeah. Just not me.

"Great! Why don't I saddle up Gandalf and Frodo tomorrow afternoon and we'll take a canter over the estate?"

"I'd love that!"

Hayley's reply sounds genuine. Like most people, she's taken immediately to Letty. I'm kind of jealous of the two of them riding off all afternoon.

One look at Hayley's exhausted face and it's clear she's ready to crash. My gaze moves over to Mother, whose poker face is in danger of cracking under the strain. I'm going to need to sweet talk the whole idea of having these guests under our roof if her frosty attitude has any hope of thawing.

After dinner, Letty accompanies Hayley to the living room to show her new piano, so I decide to check up on the office work I missed. When I reach the stairwell, Ken is coming down. He blocks my path with an outstretched foot against the bannister.

"Alex, what are they really doing here? What's going on?"

"Lawson needs protection," I say in a low voice. "She's part of the package. Don't worry about it."

He nods. "Mother's not happy."

"Yeah, what's new?"

"I suppose it's your dick doing all the thinking as usual?"

"What's that supposed to mean?"

"Here's what it means." Ken comes closer so I can count all the worry lines that really shouldn't be on a twenty–three–year–old's forehead. "When it's clear Seb's not coming back and your job here is actually permanent, that yes, you do actually have to run the business, and you'll never see your chopper again, you're going to bolt, aren't you? I think these schemes of yours—the stupid Saudi wedding and now *this*—are your over–the–top way of saying 'don't expect too much from me.'"

"I'm glad you have it all figured out," I say.

"You'll run. Maybe not today, maybe not tomorrow, but some day. And then who'll it be? Me? Letty?" He laughs. "I don't think so."

"Seb *will* come back."

"Alexander?" Mother calls from the drawing room before I head upstairs.

Crap.

Ken flashes me a smug look and saunters off.

"Mother." I loiter in her doorway, tapping my hand against the doorframe. "You look wonderful."

"Sit down here and stop pandering."

I sigh. Entering the warm room, I take a place on her sofa and pretend not to see the tablet where she's been playing online poker again.

"These people." She gives a practiced shudder and pulls out her knitting needles from a basket by her side. She's knitting this hideous, gray scarf that each of us is dreading is for us. "How long are we to be graced by their presence?"

"Not long. Just until Friday. Why?"

"I'm looking forward to having the place to ourselves, that's all. It's bad enough Ken wanting to open up for more public days without inviting people into our private sphere as well."

"I never agreed to more public days. Ken answers to me, Mother."

"Nobody doubts that, darling." She reaches for her ball of wool and starts winding up a loose end, never taking her eyes off me. "Now. Is it true you're not piloting anymore?"

"No, I'm taking a break."

Her look is appraising. "I know this has all been very sudden for you. Your plans have been rudely interrupted, as have everyone's. I know you miss Sebastian terribly. Don't we all?" She sighs heavily. "But shacking up with the latest actress from America is hardly the cure to your troubles."

"Artist, Mother, not actress."

Her eyelids droop like there's no distinction there she can be bothered figuring out. Her knitting resumes at double pace. "Alexander, you're the duke now, whether you like it or not. The world is watching you. As a dowager duchess I'm telling you that you simply can't afford to take the same liberties as you've been doing up to now."

When I don't answer, she says in a feeble tone, "It feels so chaotic here without Sebastian."

She's obviously overheard my argument with Ken on the stairs. I pat her hand. "Yeah. I know." She's not a touchy–feely mother so I let her hand go. I'd be lying if her assessment of "chaotic" didn't sting, even if it's kind of true.

Despite Seb not being her biological son, he's her clear favorite, and he's ironically the one most like her—determined, calculating, melancholic. She could have rejected him when, as a newlywed, a strange baby was unceremoniously dumped on Father, but I'd say abandoning that baby never even occurred to her. I was told by Mrs. B that they had some weird bond from the beginning.

Mother took Seb in as one of her own even though he was conceived around the same time as she'd started dating Father "exclusively." Maybe that term was used more flexibly in the nineties. She always stuck up for him as he grew up—we were never allowed to tease him—and she protected his identity fiercely even when the press hounded them for photos of the heir. But when they somehow uncovered the truth ten years ago, Father was forced to change his mind about succession. That was when my face started appearing on websites and newspaper articles all over the place. Nobody seemed to mind that, least of all me. I was a sixteen–year–old getting a lot of female attention.

Mother straightens her back and attacks a new line of stitches with determined speed. "Where were you going anyway? Don't let me stop you."

## 11

HAYLEY

I learned to ride when I was seven, tagging along behind a horse–obsessed cousin. I kept it up regularly until I was twelve. That training served me well today. Riding with Letty was wonderful. We took off, her on Gandalf—a large, four–year–old gray stallion and me on Frodo, a slightly smaller brown two–year–old. We galloped across acres of rolling, grassy countryside, which Letty informed me is all part of the Belgrave estate. I can't pretend I'm not impressed.

I haven't seen Alex or Uncle Stig all day and it's helped swing my mood back to a tentative normality. It's therapeutic, being here with Letty in the stables, unbridling, getting the horses ready for the night after our ride. The pungent stench of old manure and the rituals of brushing and sweeping help to calm my nerves. Low sunlight streams in through the leafy trees, bathing everything in dappled light—golds, bronzes, and dusty pinks. No wonder the impressionist school of painting started in Europe. My uncle was right on one point. It's not good for an artist to stay in one place, under the same sky, all the time.

Letty pauses in brushing down Gandalf's mane. "Mother wants me to marry Peter Maxwell, you know." She throws back her head, laughs showing all her perfect teeth.

"Who's he?"

"An Earl from Gloucester with a big trust fund. Frightfully clever chap."

"Well, that's good?"

"He's about as exciting as that bale of straw you're sitting on."

"Oh." I'm wrapping a blade of straw around my ring finger, pretending it's gold, trying to tuck in the end so it looks neat. "Do you want to marry him?"

"Not particularly."

My head darts up. "Well, why does your mother want you to?"

"Oh, he's rich. I may even do it, you know." She hums an aimless tune.

She reaches down and pats my arm. "Don't look so shocked, Hayley. The aristocratic way is to marry for money and take a lover for love. My parents just got lucky that there was actually some affection there too." She laughs. "Purely accidental."

"But surely nobody needs to marry for money nowadays?"

"I like this lifestyle." She waves around at the stables, the sheds, and the fields and sighs. "I'll never make money from my piano. And I don't want to help my brothers with the tedious eco–farming accounts all my life. Alex says I shouldn't forget that."

"Really?"

"Yes, he says I'm the most likely to marry into money and that I shouldn't waste any opportunities, as no man will ever be good enough for me anyway. You may see us as rich, Hayley, but we have cashflow problems like anyone else. Actually, ours are much bigger. The taxes alone are insane. I try not to think about it too much." She returns to brushing Gandalf's mane with extra vigor.

My mind jumps to the paintings in the living room, the Louis XIV table, the elaborate candelabras on the dining room table, the countless gold furnishings, are they too attached to them to sell? Although that would only be a short–term solution, of course.

I'm staring into the distance through the window when I see someone coming toward us—a man strolling up the path from the house. Even from here I recognize Alex's gait. His jacket is tossed over one shoulder and his sleeves are rolled up to the elbows. Designer sunglasses round off the model photoshoot look. He looks like he means business. My breath catches. I rise from my bale, hastily rip the childish straw ring off my finger and crush it under my boot.

"Enjoy your ride, ladies?" he asks, peeking in the stable door. He drapes his blazer over the fence outside and stares out into the same scene I've been admiring all afternoon.

"Why don't you join us next time?" Letty sings out.

"I'll think about it. Anyway, Letty, your rehearsal." Alex nods back to the castle. "Your tutor's sitting in the hall, twiddling his thumbs."

"Crikey." Letty glances at her watch, drops the brush into a bucket and swipes straw from her riding jacket.

"The poor boy. I must leave you." She glances between us both, with a knowing smile. "Try to behave yourselves while I'm gone."

"You just focus on not murdering the Polonaise," Alex says.

"Oh, like you'd be able to tell?" She slaps her brother on the shoulder, throws me a wink as she dashes down the path to the castle.

I'm sorry to see her go. But it's exciting to be left alone again with her brother. This time, I can think straight. I've met all his family and they're good people. Well, as far as I can tell, even if some of them are less than welcoming.

"I'm sure she plays the Polonaise well," I say, just to say something as I join him standing by the fence.

He turns and smirks. I'm mere inches apart from this hunk who's taller, stronger, more beautiful than anyone I've ever been with. My reflection wavers in his sunglasses, with my fly–about hair burnished red in the sunlight. I lower my gaze to the tendons in his thick neck, the angle of his jaw. Just being near him sets my skin prickling, hot and cold flushing through my body as I remember his touches on the stairs. "Look, I wanted to say ... I wanted to say thank you."

He inches his fingers along the fence until it makes contact with my little finger. I flinch away and swallow nervously. Then, I slowly move my hand back into position, making contact with him again to show him I'm not intimidated.

"Thank you for ...?" he murmurs.

I meet his eyes. "Thank you for getting Uncle Stig and me out of danger. For taking us on and making it okay with your family. Of course, it was the least you should have done, but I'm still glad you did ... although I'm not sure what your mother and Ken make of us." I round up my breathy speech with a nervous laugh.

His whole hand now cups over mine, big, strong, and warm. "You're welcome. Now, tell me what you want."

"What I want?" I blink in confusion.

"Yes. What do you want?"

It's not what I'm expecting. I take a step back, out of his grasp, glancing at the castle. Maybe it's time I got back inside.

He steps forward, clasps my upper arms and maneuvers me up close so that my nipples graze his hard torso. My body tightens. I'm overpowered. I breathe in his scent, intoxicating. I can't think. Do I want this? I let my eyes close and tilt my head up. With his whole body leaning in to me, his head angled so the sunset cuts triangles of orange into his cheeks, his gaze so intent on me as if I'm the only creature in the world, he's hard to resist. My mouth slackens as I flutter my eyes open again.

"You want me to kiss you?" His voice rasps in my ear, his breath cool on my burning cheeks. He steps back, letting go. He doesn't want it?

Angry tears spring up in the backs of my eyes. I'm burning with indignation. I've read this one wrong, so horribly wrong. How could I be so dumb?

He's turned his back to me to lean over the fence, gazing out at the fields. After a minute that feels like an hour, he speaks again. "The vibe I'm getting from you is that you'll let me do things to you, not that you *want* me to do them. Don't get me wrong, I'd do those things to you and much more." His voice is rougher, raspier. He swings around to face me again.

I'm glad he can't hear my heart.

"But I have to be sure. I find it very difficult to read you."

His vivid, blue eyes glint in the low sunlight. As his gaze roams over my hardened breasts, I feel as exposed as if he'd just ripped off my clothes. Down below, I'm wet. But he doesn't—or shouldn't—know that. I'm hot. I'm confused. I wish I knew how to play this game.

He gives me a smile that lifts up only one side of his mouth. "If you need me, you know where I am." He turns and tramps the same way as his sister toward the castle without a backward glance.

# 12

HAYLEY

It's another sunny day here in Belgrave Castle, my strange new home. I've spent an hour in the library with a book on my lap, gazing out the window as the gardener mows perfect lines around the duck pond and all the way down to the rose garden. When the roar of the lawn mower dies down, I pack up my sketching gear to go outside and join Uncle Stig and the dowager duchess, who are loitering in the herb garden out back. I may as well do something constructive with my time.

The Duchess's smile withers as I step outside on to the patio. I know she's in mourning and bound to be a little morose if she did love her late husband as Letty claimed, but there's something else bubbling under the surface. I've sat through two family dinners with her at this point and she's watched me with her navy blue hawk eyes, as if she expects me to run away with the family silver stashed under my coat.

I'd like to reassure her that I have zero interest in sponging off them a second longer than necessary. What I actually say is, "Oh, what a beautiful garden. Did I hear you saying you were going to plant Wisteria?"

"Indeed, we shall," comes her clipped answer.

"Good." I clasp my hands in front of me and look to my uncle. "Getting any ideas for your garden at home, Uncle

Stig?"

"I wouldn't attempt to recreate this splendor, my dear. Lady Belgrave was just about to take me to the local garden center so we can expand this section here." He points to a bald patch in the shrubbery.

"It's an impromptu decision of your uncle's," she qualifies, as if spontaneity is untoward and something she would never suggest. "We're waiting for George."

Before long, George totters up across the gravel, pulling at his hat. He's rescued me from having to make more conversation.

Uncle Stig draws me by the arm away from Lady Belgrave and George. When he seems satisfied that we're out of earshot, he turns to me, patting his forehead with his handkerchief. "Hayley, I have to meet somebody in London. I can't fly home with you on Friday after all."

"What?"

"Shhh, keep your voice down. I can't stay here any longer like a prisoner. I have private business to attend to that the duke doesn't know about and really shouldn't know about. It's none of his business, or his cronies' either. What I need you to do is relax, enjoy your stay here and just go home Friday, as planned. Your flight's booked and transport arranged. I've enlisted private security. You'll be safe. I only ask that you take my luggage with you. Re–pack it yourself so you can be sure of the contents, for security. It's just my small leather case. I've all I need here." He pats his overcoat which does seem to be bulging in the pockets.

"Hayley, it's important. I can't stay here another day."

"Will you be okay?" I ask.

"Yes." My uncle slides me a look. "Although I do regret pulling you away from here."

"What do you mean?"

"I'm sure you wouldn't be opposed if I postponed your flight another few days or even weeks?" He grins at me slyly.

"Uncle Stig, I'm going home on Friday. That's it. End of story."

He shakes his head. "Don't you see this is a fabulous opportunity? You're surrounded by art. You should be in heaven. And the duke— I've seen the way he looks at you."

My face flames up. "You've got it all wrong. He doesn't— I mean, there's nothing going on. I'll be more than glad to get on that plane on Friday."

"Hm, maybe you just need me to get out of your way. Think about it. Do you really want to go back to Laxby empty–handed after all this? Do you want to eke out a miserable existence as a part–time waitress while you paint in your attic for anyone who'll throw ten bucks your way at the next county fair? You owe it to yourself and your intelligence to seize opportunities when they come handed to you on a silver plate."

Before I can protest, Lady Belgrave approaches us.

When they've driven off for the garden center, I sink down on a bench and ponder it all. Why couldn't he just hang on until Friday and leave with me, like we'd planned? Does he really have business, or is this just some last–ditch matchmaking attempt to get me closer to the duke? It wouldn't surprise me.

Uncle Stig is like a dog with a bone when it comes to these ideas of his—ideas he's convinced will raise my standing in the world in some way. That was how I ended up in London on this trip in the first place, despite all Dad's misgivings. And it doesn't matter whose feelings get hurt along the way, because in Uncle Stig's books, the end always justifies the means.

I'm pacing around the patio when a deep voice interrupts my thoughts. "Where's everyone? Where's your uncle?"

It's Alex. But I'm in not in the mood to talk to him. "Oh." I wave a vague hand. "Garden center."

He swings around to look at the parking lot, eyebrows drawn tight together. "When did they leave?"

"I don't know. Maybe half an hour ago?"

"You *let* him go?"

I finger a Rosemary plant and bend to smell its fragrance

before answering. "I didn't realize I was supposed to keep him locked up."

"Which garden center?"

"I don't know, Alex. They said a local one."

He pulls out his phone and shoves it at me. "Call him."

"Why?"

"Mother doesn't carry a phone and George won't take a call when he's driving."

"No, I mean why should I call him at all?"

"I need to know what he's up to."

"Alex, he's a grown man," I say in my most sensible voice. It feels good to know something he doesn't.

His gaze moves from my face to my hand on his arm, which I don't remember putting there. I don't withdraw. I give his flesh a tiny squeeze. "Please, Alex, don't worry. Looks like he's done your mother some good, actually. They've been laughing a lot this afternoon."

His eyes flash warmly. "Yes, yes, I noticed that."

"And you can't control everything," I say. I love how his eyelids are fluttering, like this is catching him somehow off guard, like I actually might have some power over him after all. It makes me feel incredible.

"So ..." I inch my fingers forward on his arm, brushing the soft hairs. God, he feels beautiful, strong, smooth, warm. But most beautiful of all is his rapt attention to what I'm doing to him. "Why don't you go back to work, and I'll deal with Uncle Stig?"

He traps my hand on his arm with his. "Hayley, he probably thinks he's got a better way to sort out his mess than waiting around here. And he's probably right. But he's wrong to go off with no protection at all. Don't you understand?" His blue eyes blazing into me are hampering my ability to understand anything.

"We need to get him back. Trust me."

I take one look at the seriousness of his face and I do trust him. Alex has the same kind of connections that my uncle does, and I suspect he understands the vagaries of the game

Uncle Stig is playing with the Azerbaijanis. "Well, what can we do?"

Alex is already dialing a number. "Hi, Hargreaves? Yes, this is Alex Belgrave. Yes. Terribly sorry, but is my mother there by any chance? Uh–huh. Oh they did? Alright. No, that's perfectly fine. Yes, yes. Goodbye."

He clicks with his tongue as he closes the call. "Tell me where you think he might have gone after the garden center. Any haunts he'd feel safe in?"

I shrug. "I have some ideas. But they're all in London."

"Right, let's go to London."

"Uh, when?"

"Now."

## 13

ALEX

I don't normally drive this fast, but Lawson's got a head start on us and he could be anywhere in Greater London. We're in the Aston Martin, strongest engine I own, apart from my chopper. I was tempted to fly, but God knows where I'd be able to land and we may lose more time in the end.

I watch Hayley in the passenger seat out of the corner of my eye. She's clinging to her armrest, gazing out the window as we duck and weave on the A and B roads to London—I refuse to do the M25. We're whizzing past small villages, remarking on this or that, but not really talking. I'm grateful for the silence. My mind's on overdrive. Deep down I know I probably shouldn't be doing this at all. It's probably not my business if her uncle decides to take matters in his own hands. But to leave Hayley stranded, potentially at the mercy of irate Azerbaijani businessmen? *This* I take personally.

The sun is setting as we pass the outer perimeter of London. Twenty minutes later I announce—before the sat nav can do it— "We're coming up to Gordon's." I slow down in a leafy, pedestrian street with elms spilling over high, wrought–iron gates. "Reckon he's in there?

"It's my first guess," she says. "He's always talked about it fondly. But it's members only—they're very strict. You won't get in."

I slide her a look.

She shrugs. "What?"

"I'm the Duke of Fernborough. I'll get in."

She rolls her eyes. "Fine. Don't let my plebeian insecurities trip you on your way out."

I laugh and jump out. There's one doddery old gatekeeper on the door who recognizes me on sight and who attended Father's funeral last month. Not only am I admitted entrance, they practically fall at my feet with gratitude for gracing their doorstep.

The club is a standard, gentleman's club outfit, musty old furniture, stuffy service, a little shabby all round, to be honest. There's no uncle. After a few minutes of useless chit–chat about Father's death, the Windsors, and staunch refusal of tea or brandy, I leave the gaggle of grandpas and their nicotine–clogged air and escape back to the car. The freshness of her rose scent filling the interior is like heaven to my nostrils.

Her eyebrows quirk up. "So, they just let you in."

"The problem isn't getting in, darling, it's shaking these people off again."

She's rubbing her forehead, trying not to smile. "Unbelievable."

"Come on." I rev up the engine. "What's number two?"

"Well, I've ordered them geographically, radiating out from ground zero, which is here," she says, all business. "Next stop, Parsons Green. There's another one there."

"Order them by likelihood."

"I don't know him that well, Alex."

"Read out your list then, by category, not by name."

"Club, club, bowling alley, restaurant, railway station," she rattles off.

"Think about it. Where would you go to hide if you thought a crazy duke was after you?" I ponder aloud.

"Bowling alley!" we shout in unison.

"Reverse," she shrieks, jabbing the button for the navigation. She's already stored them all in. Smart woman.

And if I'm not mistaken, she's enjoying this as much as I am.

This is what makes her so different to every woman I've ever dated. They'd be more preoccupied with whether their makeup is perfectly applied, and their clothes sitting right. What am I saying? They wouldn't even dream of coming on a trip like this with me in the first place.

I've spent far too much of my free time strutting around with such women from function room to club, to VIP arena in various sporting venues, bored out of my mind with an empty feeling in my stomach, providing fodder for the next day's society blogs and gossip columns. Hayley doesn't have a shred of pretension in her and I want more of this, this feeling, this sensation that life is really happening and it's somehow important and worthwhile and natural and warm and real.

I look over at her. She's back to gripping the armrest again like it's going to save her life. "What's up?"

She lets out a ragged breath. "You know those round signs with the numbers on them? We call them speed limits in our country."

"Don't worry." I grin at her. "I don't get speeding tickets."

"No?"

"I have an understanding with Her Majesty's constabulary."

"Well, that'll sure help if we crash."

"You should see me in the air," I mutter, and instantly regret it. I didn't mean for that to come out. But she's devouring me with those curious, hazel eyes, eyes that have to know everything.

After a pause, she says, "You're a pilot?"

"I was. Not anymore."

"Do you miss it?"

"No," I grind out. It's such a lie. But I don't want to get into all this. To her, I'm a duke. The duke. The duke who's going to get her home safely, without hassle. Not some joker helicopter pilot.

"What about you?" I ask, deliberately accelerating so she'll peel her eyes off my face. "Is what you do what you want to do? I mean, your art?"

"Oh yes, art is my life. Always has been. I never wanted to study anything else. I want to be one of those lucky people who manage to make a living from it. Uncle Stig says I need to put more time into making connections, though, if I'm to have any chance of making a difference in today's world."

She looks down and fiddles with her handbag. I can't examine her face because I'm driving, but my general impression is that she doesn't look happy.

"What, like your uncle?" I say, lightheartedly. "Don't go there."

"I like the way you think about my career." She sighs heavily. "The alternative to making connections, though, is making pitiful money from doing artist in residences, workshops for middle–class children, or trying to sell my work online. But at least I'd be creating art."

"What about teaching?"

"Yeah, I've met a few teachers. If I work with primary or secondary kids, I'll be too exhausted to do any of my own work until I retire. If I get into higher education, I may get to spend free research time making art for a very small audience. But if I'm unlucky, I'll end up writing meaningless papers on subjects no one's interested in and eventually I'll end up bitter, twisted and hating everyone around me."

I laugh at her mock tragic tone. "So much to look forward to."

She laughs, too. I'm starting to get hooked on that lyrical sound and I'm keen for her to do it more. "Well, maybe the best thing to do is to not get into that mindset in the first place. Make art because it makes you happy and is important to who you are. You don't need to be recognized by an elitist system that's only interested in making money to make your work real."

She's quiet now. "Easy for you to say. You're *part* of the elitist system."

"Yeah," I concede. While we struggle with budgets and

income, we are inarguably wealthy by almost anyone's reckoning. If we were to sell off all our assets, it would amount to billions. I don't know about rent prices, or insurance fees. I couldn't say what a pint of milk costs.

As she watches me, I have to bite my tongue to prevent myself offering her something, anything, to help her in her life. I know she wouldn't want that and I admire that in her. A silence overcomes us, but it's strangely comfortable.

"We're here," I say, as I draw up under the neon bowling alley signs. "It's getting late. That means he's either here or we're fucked. The radius of possibility is just too large at this stage."

"No," she says, unbuckling her seatbelt. "I'm fucked. You've done all you can."

"Will you stop talking about being fucked and get out of here?" I growl. "I mean it, I'm getting all horny again and even *I* can see it's not a good time."

A smile broadens across her face. "Are you saying you were horny before?"

I narrow my eyes. "Could you kindly pass me one of those baseball caps in the glove compartment? Actually, might be a good idea if you wore one, too."

"Yeah, I keep forgetting I'm famous," she mutters, pulling on a Team Mercedes Formula 1 cap and handing me mine. I'm sure we'd look real cute if the paparazzi were around to catch us, which thankfully they're not.

"Let's do this!" I say.

We run to the entrance of the bowling alley. Inside, it's a dive, but teeming with happy folk. We're greeted by the loud rumbling of balls on wooden floors and the general cacophony of tipsy team members celebrating their strikes.

I follow her, glancing around under the shade of my cap. I get the feeling nobody in this place would recognize the US ambassador to Britain if he's here, just as they fail to recognize us. I must tell Marty that a bowling alley is the place for a clandestine meeting if he or his fellow MI6 spooks ever need one.

I hang back while she charges up and down the lanes. This is not going to work. He's not here. Lucky for him. If he were, I'd have punched him. What was so desperate about his situation in my house that he had to run off? Why couldn't he just have waited until I gave the green light?

It's all my fault for not watching him more closely. Never in a million years would I have thought he'd have the charm to rope Mother into getting George to drive him off the premises. He's a wily goat for sure. I can see where his niece gets it.

She looks so dejected, as if she was actually expecting this escapade to have resulted in success. I wrap my arm around her shoulder and lead her out to the car. "Come on, it's late. Let's just go home. And from this point on, please let me handle your security." My voice is so angry, I hardly recognize myself. I've made Hayley flinch, but it's how I feel. To my surprise, I am seriously pissed off. Anger is not a currency I usually deal in.

"I'm going home on Friday," she says in a meek voice.

"Are you?" I say. "Well, only if I say so."

No answer. Stony silence.

That silence stays with us, like an unwelcome passenger, the whole three hours back to Fernborough. A steady glow of angry concern for her burns somewhere deep inside an unreachable niche of my heart. Or is it just my stomach? We've skipped dinner and I am absolutely famished.

"Hungry?" I ask her as I park.

Her pale face staring at me makes my heart clench. "Oh, God, yes."

"Midnight snack sound good?"

There's a small smile. "Does it ever!"

## 14

HAYLEY

I have not seen inside the Belgrave kitchen before. It's functional, industrial, and very much a mix of styles and generations. A cat slinks away when we ease the door open.

"That's Sauron," he says. "Not very sociable, like his namesake."

I snort. "Are *all* creatures here named after *Lord of the Rings?*"

He gets a kind of faraway look in his eyes. "Yeah. Not my idea, though." Then he turns and gets busy pulling out bread and a board and knife.

I venture to the massive, cream–colored 1950s fridge and pull out butter and mineral water. He directs me to the ham, cheese, and tomatoes.

Turning around, my shoulder hits him in the chest. "Sorry." I step back. "I appear to be sleep walking. Jet lag, you know."

"No harm done." Alex reaches out and slides his hand down my arms, sending a delicious shiver throughout my body. I warm up, all over. How I missed his touch.

"You okay?" He takes the butter and water from my limp hands.

I nod.

He turns and chops tomatoes and butters bread with an efficiency that tells me he doesn't leave all his food preparation up to their hired cook. I sit on a stool and focus on his strong forearms, his nimble fingers, the intent look on his face. Soon he has two neatly cut sandwiches and he gestures that I grab one. I jump down and stand beside him at the kitchen island. As we munch, facing each other with our hips pressed against the island, I study the terracotta tiles, unable to hold his gaze. I've no clue what to say to him anymore. The grandfather clock in the next room chimes out eleven.

Licking crumbs off his thumb after finishing the sandwich, he finally breaks the silence. "Letty's having her piano recital tomorrow night—a small gathering in the drawing room. Would you like to come?" A glimpse of his former ease returns when he smiles broadly.

"Sure." I smile back. "If you think it's safe enough?"

"It will be. You'll find they're an extremely discreet lot."

"I can well believe it. So, what's the dress code?"

His gaze roves over me. Not quite an eye–fuck, but not far off. "Come as you are. It's not formal."

"Yeah." I glance down my stripy cotton top and jeans with the series of artful rips mid–thigh. Something tells me he doesn't mean that literally.

He's looking at the ripped jeans now, grinning. He fingers the marble tabletop. "Look. I— I'm sorry it's been frightful for you here. We're all at work most of the time, and—"

"What?" I laugh, mainly to cover up the awkwardness because *now* it feels like he's apologizing for something *else*, and if he is, then I don't know what that means—that he's finally taking me seriously? Or he's lost interest? Have I just been friend–zoned?

"It's been fun," I lie. "I helped Mrs. B with her beeswax polishing this morning—I can see why she calls it a never–ending chore—and I had a lot of fun perusing the almanacs in the library." I don't tell him I only did that to avoid the dowager duchess, who Letty told me never enters any rooms that were the special haunts of her late husband.

Alex laughs and moves in closer, as close as he can get without touching. "Hm, if that's what you call fun …"

My heart stops dead when he leans in and grazes his lips over my cheek. "You need to raise your expectations," he mutters close to my ear. Then he backs off.

*Tease.* But this time I don't mind it.

A loud scraping of furniture from upstairs breaks the spell. "I probably need to get to bed now," I say.

"Yes, you're jetlagged, and I've an early start," he says, his expression unreadable. "Need help finding your bedroom?"

*Are you offering?* I almost ask, but don't. "No, no, I think I know my way around by now."

The next morning, I wake with a feeling of unease when I think about the trouble Uncle Stig has caused, but I banish it to the back of my mind. I reckon he's able to take care of himself. It's only ten–thirty, but the house is buzzing with preparations for the recital and dinner tonight. I watch out the window as a series of delivery trucks drive up as far as they can go—a florist, a fruit and vegetables man, and a butcher.

I amuse myself by staying out of everyone's way and cataloguing all the seventeenth– and eighteenth–century art in the house, or at least in all the rooms that have open access. They're large, ostentatious, but not highly valuable, as most are lesser known artists, protégés of the famous ones. The Belgrave family portraits were all done by one family of painters, the tradition passed on from son to son, in parallel to the dukedom itself. It's all fascinating, but my hopes of chancing across a genuine Renoir or Rembrandt worth millions are dashed.

By five p.m. I go up to my room to prepare for the evening's entertainment. It's not like I need much time to prepare. My makeup is capsule–sized, and all I have to work with are a light foundation and eyeliner. I put on the most formal outfit in my suitcase—a knee–length black dress with elbow–length sleeves and a white shawl intended for a West End show with Uncle Stig. We had tickets for *Les Misérables*.

I loiter in my room until seconds before six in the hope that Alex will drop by to "show me the way," but he doesn't. As the mantelpiece clock bongs out six times, I swallow my disappointment. I guess he's busy helping with preparations.

When I enter the huge, arched doorway of the drawing room, it's like I've stepped into a Kate Middleton impersonation competition. Loitering gracefully around are women ranging from around my age to well into their thirties or forties. Maybe even fifties, but nobody here looks a day over thirty–nine with their subtle, rosé makeup and sparking eyes. They're all polished, with coordinated jewelry, belts, nude pumps and teensy clutch purses. And Alex said it wasn't formal?

It's a fashion blogger's paradise. I can imagine an off–stage commentator with a heavy English accent chirping, "And now here comes Clarissa Banville–Fowler, wearing an exquisite Victoria Beckham ensemble in darkest fuchsia, topped off to perfection with a crème bolero, yadda, yadda, yadda."

A staff of six or so waiters has magically appeared, along with white tablecloths, red–upholstered chairs, and fresh–cut flowers. The splendor would put many a wedding or ambassadorial function to shame. I'm scanning the room for Alex. But I don't see him. Champagne is flowing and it's *frightfully* good stuff, as Letty would say. I don't mind if I take a glass.

Halfway through my second glass, I feel a male presence gliding up from behind. I know just by the way the air weirdly tingles when he's close that it's him.

"You startled me," I complain, but my face breaks into a grin.

"Glad you could make it." His eyes do a rapid scan of my body, over my prim dress. Not much skin is visible but from the wolfish gleam in those eyes, I sense he's judging what's underneath all the same. "I was beginning to worry you'd got lost."

"Your castle's not *that* big."

He gives me his adorable half grin. "No one's complained about the size before."

I rest my back against the wall, trying to look nonchalant. "Oh, I'm not complaining."

It's not helping my poise that several pairs of perfectly made–up eyes are darting in my direction. I'm being assessed from all sides and there are no doubts as to which path the conversations are taking.

"What the devil did you do with yourself all day?" he asks.

"Oh, a bit of reading, bit of sketching." *A lot of snooping.*

"Busy girl."

"I need to do something with my hands."

"I could suggest something."

"Yeah, I'm sure you could."

He moves closer so I feel the warmth of his arm up against mine. "For example, you could explore my castle. Seen many castles, have you?"

My breath hitches as his fingers slide up and down the curve of my waist. "A few."

"But any as impressive as mine?"

I smile into my champagne glass. "I've seen more ruins than erect ones." I nestle my butt very deliberately into his hip. Hey, he asked for it.

"And say you … got access to one of these erect castles." His voice is hoarse. "What would you do with it?

"I'd never leave it."

"Never?" His gaze hops between my eyes and my mouth. My heart is thumping. I so want to kiss him, but not with everyone watching, and they *are* watching, damn them.

"Your Grace, so good to see you," a loud, plummy voice intrudes like a cold shower. A mid–fifties man has sauntered up, looking faintly bucolic in a baggy, tweed jacket. He has that same air of detached superiority as they all do, and just assumes he's not intruding on us, or doesn't care if he is. "I'm terribly sorry, but Lord Cavendish would like your input on the briefing for Suffolk Country Club next week."

Alex's hand falls away from me and he straightens up. "Of course." He gives me one last look that could mean anything from "have fun by yourself now" to "wait for me." And then he's gone.

Deflated, I search around the assembly for diversion. I'm not a total novice in such company, having attended a few society events with Uncle Stig. I nab another flute of champagne and do the rounds, exchanging pleasantries with any clusters of people who seem receptive. It helps that nobody mentions, or even appears to be aware of, the existence of YouTube. The "I'm a student over here to study the fine arts" story goes down as smoothly as the champagne. Nobody finds it difficult to believe that I'm taking off for a few months to visit galleries on my uncle's expense. After that, the conversations usually revert to the particulars of the duke's responsibilities, Letty's recital, or some completely boring gossip about other members of the peerage whose pretentious names sound totally made–up, except they're not.

Exhausted after an hour of it, I nab a nice spot to stand by the fireplace, where enough people are coming and going not to appear like a wallflower, and yet, I don't actually have to talk to any of them. I get to poke the fire now and again with a huge brass poker. At times, Alex looks like he's trying to make his way over to me, but then, like a swimmer getting thrown back by the waves, he keeps getting pulled over by folks interested in talking to him.

It gives me time to practice coy smiles to project at him across the room. He intercepts some of them, and when he does, he looks hungry, like a man unwilling to play games any longer. Which is good, because I'm going to launch myself at him the first moment I get a chance.

Ken saunters up and offers what appears to be a genuine smile. I return it as graciously as I can, but it puts an abrupt end to my flirting. We stand with our backs to the fire, surveying the room. He's as tall as Alex and looks strong as a horse but in a more deliberate, body–building way. I've been watching him navigate the room, and people don't gravitate toward him the way they do to Alex. With me, he seems awkward, as if he wants to say something, but can't find the words. Adorkable, if you go for that.

"Well, he's duke now." Ken finally finds his tongue.

I find his statement puzzling, so I answer as noncommittally as I can. "He certainly is."

"He's not used to it," he says.

"All the attention, you mean?"

"The everything." He turns to me sharply. "Are you enjoying your stay here?"

"Of course."

A bell chimes, relieving me of the obligation of further conversation. The usher guides people to the fifty chairs in a horseshoe shape around Letty's stage. Ken is to my left and some old gent to my right. I search for Alex, but he's up front, talking to his mother.

I listen along, rapt, to the classical piece that Letty's fingers are conjuring from the piano. I smile to myself, remembering Alex asking her not to murder the Polonaise. She's actually amazing. Not a single person has taken out a phone. You'd swear they didn't even own them. Nothing speaks for their elevated level of manners so much as this. It's like we're transported in a time machine back two centuries. I expect Jane Austen to walk in at any moment and start pithily observing people.

After the performance, I approach Letty on the stage, once her initial fan group disperses.

"So what did you think?" Her sparkling eyes are targeted at me.

"Oh my God, you were amazing."

"She's so sweet, Alex." Letty clutches onto his arm in a way that suggests she's not entirely sober, which makes her performance all the more remarkable. "Hold on to this one."

"Shut up, Letty. Hayley's—"

"An ambassador's niece." Letty flicks her hand. "That's every bit as accomplished as the sister of a royal duke, the archbishop's second cousin, or the Countess Wilcox. And so much more dignified than your Tom Ford models. I don't see why—"

"I was *going* to say she's leaving soon," he cuts in.

Oh God, Letty really is drunk. How mortifying.

"Protect your piano before one of these brats scratches it," Alex says sharply.

I turn to see some kids messing with her piano stool.

Her eyes widen. "Crap, yes."

"And Letty." Alex indicates a suave, early thirties man in a tight, cream blazer, surrounded by three ladies. "For Christ's sake, go talk to Peter before he showers his gallantry on more deserving females."

"But—" she protests.

"Now."

"Well!" She tosses her hair and marches off.

Alex turns to me as if to say something, but I hold up my hand to stop him.

"What was that?" I demand.

"What?"

"The way you talked to Letty just there. I know she's tipsy, but you can't tell her who she should talk to."

"I can tell her whom she can't afford to ignore," comes his reply.

I turn back to look at her. This must be Lord Peter Whatever, the wealthy earl from Gloucester. Letty's lavishing her attention on him as if she's never been happier to see anyone in her whole life, but all I'm thinking about is that bale of straw. She should have put up more of a fight. The guy's wiry chest puffs up under the blazer when she laughs uproariously at what he's saying and I know there is no way she actually likes that guy. But then I remember the rest of her talk in the stable. She really does want to marry for money. This I find totally depressing.

"There's fun and there's serious," Alex says solemnly, as if reading my thoughts. "If she wants fun, this is neither the time nor the place for it."

But you're allowed to have your fun—the sister of a royal duke, the archbishop's second cousin …

"Your Grace?" The annoying tweed jacket guy from before has wandered over, now with a younger woman on his arm. I say younger, but she's probably his age. I gave up trying to guess the women's ages here about two hours ago. "Terribly remiss of me not to have inquired before, but how is it going with your fine collection?"

"It's … fine, thank you." Alex's tone is few degrees cooler even than the tone he just used with Letty.

There's a super keen glint in Tweed Jacket's beady eyes. "Did you manage to root out anything in the dust?"

"Nothing of import."

"Perhaps Your Grace requires assistance in this matter? I'd be much obliged—"

"Thank you," Alex says. "Not necessary."

"I did hear a rumor about—"

A man with hipster glasses and purple bowtie emerges out of nowhere and chimes in, "Ah yes, Sir John, but *The Times* claims the Old Masters are losing relevance."

Tweed Guy nods. "Collectors aren't interested anymore. Not even the major auction houses. Maybe it's time to dust off and sell up before it's too late, Your Grace?"

As Tweedledum and Tweedledee stare him down, Alex rubs the back of his neck. I'm getting the vibe he's not used to handling this side of the family business. I don't know what he's got stashed away in those closed–off rooms and in their basement, but I'm sure that if Alex inherited it from his father, it's not just about the money. Besides, these goons are talking through their baggy, corduroyed asses.

Hipster Guy is not letting up. "The very term is a horrible piece of pretension. What does Old Master even mean?"

Sir John taps Alex's arm. "You custodians only have yourselves to blame, you know."

"I consider myself admonished," Alex says through barely

parted lips. I scuttle in closer to him for moral support.

Hipster snorts. "It's not too late to take matters into your own hands, Your Grace."

Alex's fingers curl into a fist behind his back.

I can't take this shit a second longer. I step forward, a smile plastered on my face and I don't mind laying on my thickest West Coast accent either. "From what I heard, the best Old Masters are selling for unheard of prices. Last year Rubens's Scene of Lot Being Seduced broke, what, 45 million pounds?" I turn to the hipster and glare at his horrible horn–rimmed glasses. "Of course, the media ignores this, because bashing old art is just too easy, isn't it?"

Hipster gapes at me for a full five seconds before opening his bearded lips again. "My dear girl, we hardly need the media for that. The custodians have reveled so long in intellectualism, putting on obscure exhibitions to scare off the public."

This gains a polite round of laughter from the folks gathering beside us.

"Oh, come on," I say. "Look at the Bosch show selling out in the Prado, the Goya and the Rembrandt that sold out in London, and of course the Leonardo show a few weeks back? There are better ways of encouraging folks to see the Old Masters than ranting against the curators."

A firm grip encircles my arm. Is it Alex's signal for "shut up?" He knows me well enough by now to know that I say what I mean. But I catch his eyes and they're glowing warm.

"This is Hayley. She's my art advisor."

*Ooh, art advisor.* I have to press my lips together hard to avoid laughing.

"She has firm opinions on the matter, of course," Alex continues. "I hope you appreciate our position. If not, I'd be happy to discuss. But for now, Lord Blakely, Sir John, can I interest you in some brandy from my collection?"

Hipster guy looks like someone stole his cotton candy. "Not my cup of tea, Your Grace. Do get in touch if you're thinking of moving anything around?" With a parting sneer at me, he struts off, Sir John shuffling after him.

It takes a while for my eyebrows to drop.

Alex lets out a long breath. "Thanks. Thought I'd never get rid of them. Wow, are you serious about all those shows showing interest?"

"I may have exaggerated a little," I admit. "I think the Leonardo was a few years back, not a few weeks."

He laughs. "You are something else."

"I'm curious, though," I say.

"About what?

"About the art you got stashed around there. I mean, if I'm your advisor and all."

His fingers trace a pattern on the flesh of my thumb, down and up, lulling me into silence. "You'll see the whole castle in due time," he says finally.

"Due time?" I laugh. He's made it sound like I'm here on some extended vacation. But hell, I'll play along.

Ken comes up. "Alex, you're wanted over with Gordon. Come on, it's your turn." Ken nods at an old guy in a wheelchair who must be hitting a hundred.

Alex looks at the old guy, then at me, then Ken, and then groans. "Excuse me." He walks off into the crowd, and I brace myself for more awkward conversation from his brother. From Ken's satisfied smile, it's clear that Gordon was just a ruse to break us up. It takes all my willpower not to throw my champagne over him.

# 15

ALEX

Luckily it's not just Father's art collection in the lower echelons of the castle; there's also a tunnel to our underground 25–meter, heated swimming pool. That's what I need. I need to calm down and get her off my mind.

I did my duty with old Gordon, helping him out to his car, listening to his health woes, and now they can survive without me for an hour. It was Letty's gig tonight, so I trust she can do the rest of the door duty and make sure everyone leaves feeling important. The sooner Seb's back and taking over the ceremonials again, the better, because I have no stomach for it.

There's a text from Marty telling me to call him, so I do. He tells me they located Lawson in a club in London late last night. He's safe for now, or at least, under their surveillance, and Marty advises me to stay out of it. I'm only too happy to stay out of it although I do appreciate that it gave me a chance to do something alone with Hayley, away from home. She'll be relieved to hear this news.

I'm already changed, so I dive into the water and stay under until the last second, before coming up gasping. I glide to the other end. Twenty more lengths like that and I'm calmer. Father had this pool built because he was petrified of death, petrified of his body getting a millimeter out of shape.

But it didn't help him in the end. Despite his incredibly honed fifty–eight–year–old musculature, his heart still gave out prematurely. If I die at his age, then I'm already at midlife, and I've achieved nothing. Everything I have has been handed to me—money, fame, the dukedom, the family business, and yet I can't even get on top of my basic duties, responding to the farmers' demands, reading up on legislation, pushing the business into profitability.

With every stroke of my crawl, I tell myself I'm gaining control, that everything will somehow work out, especially if I diversify our efforts away from eco–farming, which I am hopeless at, and more toward the glitzier end of business—weddings, banquets, balls, which I feel I can manage. Exhausted after forty lengths, I pull myself out of the water. I'm gripping the handles of the ladder, panting, water up to my shins, when something moves in the shadows. I spin around. Someone's there. Marty always joked that if anyone was going to kill me, it would be in this pool room—with a candlestick. I don't want to prove him right.

I leap the last two steps and grab my towel from its hook. Great weapon.

"Who is it?" I growl.

The figure emerges from the shadows and I sigh in relief. It's Hayley. She's clutching her sandals, treading barefoot toward me, slowly. Her eyes are doing a full body scan of me and I suppose there's little left to the imagination, which is unfair, because that dowdy dress covers her up in a criminal way. Her breath is coming in sharp, shallow breaths. She seems nervous.

I'm torn. I wanted to get away from her and her mixed signals, but now that she's standing before me, I'm so glad she's here. I don't know what it is with this woman. It's not classic beauty or a hard, athletic body—the things I usually go for, but every time I see her, every time she's in the same room as me, I feel more alive, and I feel that nobody else can have her. Nobody. It's a raging conviction. It makes no sense.

And when things make no sense, I fall back on humor.

"Hey, Miss Stalker, did you follow me? Are you coming to get wet?"

"No." Her gaze lands on my chest. Then my shoulders. Then my legs. My dick had shriveled from the water but is reviving under her scrutiny.

I walk toward her. "Maybe you're wet already?"

"Yes, I did follow you. And no, I'm as dry as a bone."

I grin. She's getting better at this. "So, are you checking up on me then?"

"You'd like that, wouldn't you?" Her words are soft, and I can't tell how she means them. But the fact that she's here means something.

"Maybe I would," I say in a mild tone, planting my hands on my hips.

"Truth?" she asks, her hazel eyes serious, looking up into my face.

"Please."

"I was worried. I don't know … if you were pissed off, or worried about something, just disappearing like that. You were brooding, weren't you?"

"I don't brood," I scoff.

"Oh, I think you do. You're not the playboy you try to project."

"I take offense at that." But my smile is ruining my haughty act.

"Whatever. I'm not interested in the playboy Alex. I want to know some real things about you. The *real* Alex."

I spread my arms. "At your service. Ask me anything."

"Do you miss him?"

"Whom?" I ask sharply.

"Your father. Gosh, I'm sorry, that's such a personal question."

I shake my head to indicate it's fine. "Yes, of course. He was formidable, obsessive, but a good father in the important ways—he loved my mother; he treated us kids evenly and fairly, and even if he didn't spend a lot of time with us, whenever he did, we got his undivided attention. Can't really ask for a whole lot more than that."

She nods like she understands.

"I think he always felt he'd make it up to us when he retired from the business. He wasn't to know that was never going to happen." My chest tightens because I'd never spoken this aloud to anyone before. "What about your mother? Do you remember much of her? Did she look like you?"

Hayley's quiet for a long time. Her head lowers. "Kind of. More blonde, though, more beautiful."

"Hard to imagine," I say quickly.

"Really, she was. And more talented. My memories of her are vague, though. Sometimes I don't know if they're real memories or just reconstructed from facts people have told me."

I nod and reach for her hand.

"What did your father obsess about?" she asks.

I give a short laugh. "Oh, a lot of things. But modern art mainly. Stuff that mother wouldn't allow him to hang upstairs. She calls it rubbish. It's all in the basement. Nothing valuable, unknown artists. But it made him happy to support some lesser known struggling artists."

"Collectors do get obsessive. One of them bought up my mother's entire collection anonymously." Her eyes gleam. "I wonder could it have been your father?"

"Not possible," I laugh. "Though it's a lovely theory. No, Father always put his name conspicuously to all of his purchases. So, what were her paintings like?"

"Neo–impressionist, vibrant, apparently," she says in a wistful voice.

"Apparently?"

"I've never seen them."

"What?" I recoil in surprise and drop her hand.

"No."

"Huh."

Why does she assume her mother was more talented? I don't ask, though. I trust her gut feelings on this and there's no point in rubbing it in.

"So, you're just going to stand there freezing, are you?" she asks.

"No. I'm going to do this." I bend down toward the pool, scoop up a handful of water and throw it at her. She shrieks, so I do it again because it's fun.

"Oh look, it's Countess Wet T–shirt again," I say. "Except it's a dress." The dress clings to her now like a second skin— a definite improvement. "I already guessed what you'd got going on under the dress even when it was dry, but this is so much better."

I'm chest to chest with her now by the edge of the water. She's heaving. Hell, I'm heaving. Her eyes are huge pools of flickering light from the water's reflections. She looks like there are a million things flitting through her mind, not all of them conclusive. But me, I'm thinking clearly. I know what I want.

She puts her hand flat on my abdomen. It's warm. Her head tilts up to greet my eyes.

Pretty much … that.

My cock springs to life with a hallelujah chorus. There's no hiding in these swimming briefs anyway. But she's still staring intently into my eyes, whispers of words starting to form on her lips.

"I'm—" She stops and can't seem to finish.

I raise my brows at her. The most plausible continuations are "pregnant" or "a virgin," neither of which I want to hear right now.

Her hand moves down to my lower abdomen. "Begging— "

I gape at her in speechless surprise as her eyebrows twitch and her fingers trace the skin above the rim of my shorts.

"You."

Her eyes fill with wickedness and the tip of her tongue protrudes a fraction outside her lips. *Oh mother of all that's holy.*

Before any of my limbs can react appropriately, there's a pressure against my sternum, so forceful that I have to step back to counter it. It's her hand. She's pushing me. Hard. My foot grapples for tile but find only air and then I'm toppling backward. With a blast of cold, I fall shoulder first into the water. I stay under for a few seconds, absorbing the shock of sudden cold, bubbles percolating from my nose and mouth, planning my revenge.

I swim to the ladder and shimmy up, not taking my eyes off her. She hasn't moved. She's got this goofy look of dread and amusement. Adorable. And she's got nowhere to go.

With every step of my approach, she sinks back farther toward the wall.

"You're going to pay for that," I say, and I like how it comes out rumbling and serious.

She giggles. "Oh?"

Her back's right up against the wall now, her eyes glowing through the dark.

"No escape."

She smirks back. "You win." Her eyelids flutter as I lean in.

My damp fingers graze down her neck and down to her hard nipples. I squeeze one through the damp fabric. A whining sound comes from deep in her throat. I capture her mouth with mine and use my tongue to open her jaw wider. Even though I'm being rough, there's no resistance, so I take her wrists and pull her tighter against my body. Let her share the wetness, a preview to how it'll be when I toss her in the water, too.

As our mouths and tongues collide, my hands smooth all over, wanting to know every part of her. I don't even care about revenge now, I have to have her, to drive her to ecstasy, to mark her as mine.

Our groans echo out in the stillness. Water drips from my hair and trickles between our noses. I don't know whether it's water or sweat or whether I'm shivering from lust or from the damp. Goosebumps spring up all over me. Her rosy perfume mingles with the chlorine from the water and all of a sudden, I'm sixteen again. I hold a handful of her wet hair and squeeze droplets of water onto her shoulder. The tiny stream trickles down over her collarbone and I chase it with my tongue. Her breath accelerates.

But then I hear a low thud. It's the door to the tunnel. *Christ.*

"I hear someone."

She nods. "Yeah, I hear it."

"Hayley, I need to grab my clothes from the locker. Quick, you go out that door and meet me at the other end."

"I don't care. Let them find us."

"Please—go!" The urgency in my voice makes her skitter across to the door.

# 16

HAYLEY

A passageway of low doors unfolds in front of me, long, slightly crooked, musty smelling. Alex told me to go to the end.

Halfway down, he still hasn't come out from the pool room. Curiosity wins out and I slow down to a halt, getting my bearings in the dim light. I turn the door handle of the room directly to my left, and to my surprise, it gives way, easily but with a groan. I tiptoe in.

It's a long, rectangular room, cool and with a damp, musty smell of lack of use. Through the gauze–curtained windows near the ceiling, I see roots of a bush. We're half underground. I proceed to the center of the room. The carpet is red and faded. The walls are wallpapered in dark green and adorned with intricate gold light–fittings. I search for a switch. There's a bronze panel by the door. I go back and pull the lever down. Yes, it works.

Then I see. I really see. Paintings—everywhere. A jumble of artists and themes. Some are hung on walls, others lie stacked against the walls, others still are unframed, lying flat or rolled up in tubes resting on the cabinets that hug the walls. It's quite a mess. All that talk upstairs about Old Masters hasn't prepared me for this. It's resolutely modern. It's like dropping into the MoMA for one of their avant–garde specials. I can smell the father's obsession clearly.

I'm drawn to the most striking exhibit, a massive–as–hell El Greco–esque painting of the Madonna, but painted in garish pinks and yellows. And framed in ruby red. It's so ostentatious, I let out a gasp of awe. The contrast between this bunch and the rest of the house couldn't be more startling. I can understand why the dowager duchess was appalled.

The temperature in here is a little too warm, and a tad too moist, not ideal conditions for oils or charcoals, but at least it doesn't look like the sunlight would directly hit any of the pictures. I examine them, one after the other. There are some I've heard of before—painters famous enough to be on the radar of art students, but most I've never seen before.

The door squeaks open. I gasp and fling around. It's Alex, watching me silently. He's thrown on clothes but looks damp.

"I'm sorry, I ..." I blurt. I feel super guilty like I'm an art thief caught red–handed. "I got curious. The door was unlocked."

He slams the door behind him with his foot. He turns the key in the lock. "Not any more."

"H–how long have these been hanging here?" I ask, pointing to the nearest painting.

He crosses the floor separating us with determined steps. "Anything between one and eighteen years. Father got serious about collecting on his fortieth birthday. You're practically salivating ... And it's not at the paintings, is it?"

I take a mock swipe at him. He's right. The greatest treasure in this house is standing right before me with a smarmy smile on his perfectly sculpted face, and I'm unable to believe my luck. "Come on then, show me your hidden treasures and I'll tell you what they're worth."

He takes my hand and presses it to his chest. "Let's start chronologically, in the caveman era."

He bends his head down. I reach out with my tongue to touch his. The moment we connect, the kiss explodes. His arms tighten, drawing me hard against him. His mouth is hungry and moves against mine in a kiss so blatantly possessive, so claiming, it would hurt me if it didn't feel so perfect. Then Alex lifts me. I wrap my legs around his waist as he carries me over to a large table.

"This is what I should have done the first night you stayed here." He sets me down on the hard surface and lets out a low growl. "Unzip your dress."

At his order and his hot, blazing eyes on me, a rush of heat hits between my legs. Normally I don't like being bossed around, but because it's Alex, I'm not even thinking. With shaking hands, I slowly reach around and unzip the back. I lower the zipper, relishing the way his eyes flare at the rasp of metal.

"Slide it off," he says.

I do it. The dress falls to my waist, exposing my black lace bra.

"All the way."

I maneuver my hips so that my skirt pushes down. Luckily, I've got matching black panties on, no Hello Kitty tonight. I'd like to pretend it wasn't planned, but it totally was.

"Now the rest," comes his voice, low and insistent.

I want to be naked for him. I don't care anymore about long–term repercussions. I just need whatever is coming next, and he seems to need me to do it this way for him. I unhook my bra as quickly as my fingers allow and cast the garment aside.

"Everything," he says.

When the panties are down far enough, a final wiggle makes them drop to the ground. I wait, the tension winding my belly tight. He's silent and moving, just a shadow on the gilded wallpaper, looming over me. I'm starting to feel exposed.

"Now ..." His voice is low, insistent, coaxing. "Lie back."

The polished wood surface of the table is cool against my

heated skin. Staring at the ornate ceiling of the gallery, I feel like an exhibit in his private gallery. But again, he's silent and as I wait, my core is getting wetter, more needy. My nipples draw together; my entire body readies itself for him. When I feel a finger land on the inside of my right knee, tracing a line up my inner thigh, I know what to do.

With a groan of abandon and pleasure, I open my legs. The stroke of his tongue following the path of his finger is sheer torture. He's so close to touching me where I need him the most. I open my legs wider, making it clear what I want. He doesn't make me wait. His tongue comes down flat on my clit, pressing, tasting, wrenching a high–pitched sound from me as my head lolls backward.

I've never had a man who knows what he's doing take me like this before. Alex isn't going to back off, saying it tastes weird. He's going to eat me until I come. Just the thought of that twists the tension inside of me a notch tighter.

He traces a finger around my wet folds, murmuring, "And after I taste you, I'm going to fuck you."

I hear myself saying, "Please, Alex," as he sucks my clit into his mouth and drives a finger inside me. His finger doesn't totally stretch me, but it's enough to make me feel full. His mouth's moving on me, sucking, licking as he adds another finger. I squirm and rock, wanting to thrust against his whole body, craving his cock inside me, filling me.

He teases me further. I gather he's reading my body, understanding my responses better than I can. An expert. Of course he is. Again and again, he plays me, bringing me to the edge of what I can bear, leaving me gasping, pleading before backing off again, denying me. He only lifts his head once to say, "Play with your nipples, Hayley."

I hesitate, but he gives me such a heartfelt, pleading smile that my reservations crumble. I've never done this before, but there's no way I'm refusing him anything now. I'm way too far gone. Lifting a trembling hand from the cool tabletop, I trace my fingertips around my nipples, tentatively, then harder, shivering at the twinges of pleasure.

His tongue licks me, pressing into my swollen clit, applying just the right amount of pressure. My hips surge up to his mouth, unafraid to ask. My fingers pinch harder as my body loses control.

The orgasm rips through me and my pussy clamps for dear life around Alex's fingers. He fucks me harder with them, sucking at my clit, dragging out my waves of pleasure until I need to gasp in breaths.

When I come back to myself, Alex is sitting on top of the table too, cradling me in his arms. I'm still woozy from coming so hard. Through the haze of bliss, I lift my face to his, seeking his touch. I taste myself on his lips.

He looks down at me indulgently. "You okay, Countess?"

"Yes. No." Because even though I've come harder than I thought I could, I'm now massively aware of his hard cock under my ass and I want it inside of me. And I know it's what he wants, too. I reach for him.

"More?"

I nod.

"Absolutely. But not here." He grabs me in his arms, lifts me, strides across the gallery, unlocks and kicks open the door and carries me up the stairs, naked, in the darkness. I gasp when I realize what he's doing, but he shushes me. "Nobody uses these stairs."

"I don't care. I'm naked, you idiot." I clutch onto his damp shirt with a vise grip.

"I'm fully aware of that."

I cringe and close my eyes, imagining all kinds of embarrassing scenarios, and only reopen them when he lays me gently on cool, satin sheets. As I loll there on his ginormous bed, trembling with anticipation, he grabs a condom from a drawer in the bedside table. Of course, this is why he needed to come up here.

He's naked in seconds, and seconds later, sheathed and pressing his thick cock inside my swollen pussy. I thought his fingers had filled me, but this is so much more. His cock stretches me in a satisfying, mind–numbing way and I love it.

I'm clinging to his hips for all I'm worth, moving him deeper inside of me with every thrust.

Very soon, I feel the urgent need to come and I can tell he's ready, too. I'm gasping his name as I go wild under his body, thrashing into a blind ecstasy. He surrenders to his orgasm, groaning my name and then collapses, shuddering, beside me. He rolls over and pulls me on top so I'm sprawled on his chest.

My mind goes off to happy la–la land as I look into his sultry eyes. I brush back hair from his forehead, sinking my fingers into its softness. The heaving of his chest slows down and he closes his eyes. I examine his beautiful, resting face. I'm in new territory … sated, but raw. Different. I don't know what any of this means. My thoughts are wispy clouds, hard to catch hold of. All I know is, this feels damn good.

His fingertips trace lazy circles on the base of my spine as if to tell me he's still awake but doesn't want to talk or open his eyes. I so get that. I want to stay in this position forever, just feeling, looking, breathing.

He finally says. "I knew you'd drive me wild."

My body's so relaxed, I doubt I'll ever be able to move it again. Because this is, hands down, the best sex I've ever had. He's just raised the bar to impossible heights. I know I'll regret it sometime, but not right now.

When the wooziness passes and my surroundings come into sharper focus, I'm bracing myself for some kind of anti–climax, but judging by Alex's beaming face, and the way he can't keep his hands off my body, he's feeling the same way as I am—giddy, excited.

"You hungry?" he asks.

"Among other things," I murmur. "Okay, yes." We skipped dinner, after all. But who needs food?

"I'll go pick up some scraps from the kitchen then. Wait here." Alex pulls on trousers and a shirt and wags his forefinger at me. "Don't move."

I'm laughing, shaking my head, as he bounds out the door. Why does he think I'd move? I'll never be able to move again.

He'll always be a sex god to me. I'll live here on this massive bed forever.

I lose track of time, lolling against the pillows, dreaming. At last he returns with a large silver tray and a triumphant smile. Out of "scraps" he's managed to concoct an amazing supper of salmon pastries, avocado dip, crudités, and tiny strawberry shortcake tarts. Everything tastes melt–in–the–mouth heavenly. I know Mrs. B should take the credit for the food quality, but I'm loving the fact that Alex went to the effort of presenting everything so beautifully, linen napkins and all.

I hate to say it, but I feel like a princess.

We eat in comfortable silence. Alex is as hungry as I am, if his speed of demolishing his pastry is anything to go by.

"Why don't you have people in to see them? The paintings? The sketches?" I ask, munching on the strawberry tart. It's clear he doesn't have a clue what he's got down there. I don't even know what they are, for the most part, but I want to find out.

"I guess I don't think about it much, what with the funeral and the business, and … I've been busy."

"Of course," I say gently. "It's just pretty overwhelming as an art student to see all this."

He looks at me speculatively. "I suppose it must be, yes. Could you … perhaps … see yourself … you know, cataloging this lot? Or even outsourcing the task to someone you know? Maybe the local art club? See, I just don't have a clue. All I know is that the obsession took over too much of Father's time." His voice is grim.

"What? Oh my God, I'd love that," I blurt, eager to help him in any way I can. That is, until I remember it's a nonsensical idea. My heart is soaring nonetheless. It's a dream job—on paper. Imagine being the cataloguer, the *curator* even, of this collection! What an honor. I could brighten the gallery rooms up, rearrange the paintings into themes because right now … no, just no. And maybe procure more rooms to display all of them. There must be at least seventy hanging up, but I saw a lot of cabinets and rolled up paper.

He's grinning at my stunned reaction. "Come work for me. I'll pay you whatever you think is reasonable. Although I must warn you,"—his voice lowers to a sexy rumble as he smooths his thumb down my cheek—"it's not a job for the fainthearted."

I lean into his hand, playing along. "And why would that be?"

A wicked flash gleams in his eyes. "There will be some extracurricular activities expected of you."

I shut my eyes. "Alex, I'm going home tomorrow."

"Are you?" He flops back against the pillows, hands behind his head. "Why?"

"Well, I kind of have to."

His mouth is a stubborn line. "Again. Why?"

"I–I've got college. I can't stay here."

"I thought you said it didn't start until September."

"I did," I say, biting down on my lip, running through my options. "It doesn't."

"So. Stay at least until September. Or longer. Oh, by the way, I forgot to tell you yesterday, but we don't have to worry about your uncle for now because I've heard from some contacts in the foreign service that they found him in London and he's under their surveillance and, we hope, behaving himself. So, what do you say?"

I look at his eager face. The way he's saying this tells me he thinks all obstacles have been cleared. Stuffing my annoyance at Uncle Stig to the back of my mind, I open my mouth to explain how it's really not that simple. "Ale—mmmmmf." His lips press onto mine then his tongue flicks out, tasting me.

He slides the tray to the edge of the bed and tugs me back into him. My body catches fire. I wriggle against him, feeling his cock swell.

I slide down the sheets, come up on my knees between his legs to suck his cock. Alex is the first man I've wanted in my mouth and I've been wondering what he'll taste like ever since he stretched me out on the gallery table. I get my answer—he's salty and male and perfect. I want him to come in my mouth, but before that happens, he grasps me by the hips and starts fucking me again. I don't refuse him.

I lose myself even harder. Because somewhere in the last few minutes, I know I've made the decision to stay until he's had enough of me, or me of him, or until college starts, whichever happens first.

# 17

HAYLEY

I have never been much of a morning person, but this I *could* get used to. The first thing greeting my eyes is a rose—pink and perfectly defined, sitting on top of a napkin. I blink and rise up on my elbow. Alex is gone, but laid out before me on the duvet is the same tray as last night but adorned with fragrant, fluffy croissants and a pot of what smells like tea, along with a tiny jug of milk and a cute little silver dish of thinly sliced lemon. I eye the spread greedily. I must've burned a million calories last night, so I'm good.

I can't remember the last time I drank tea and I'm wondering whether I'd prefer to drink it with milk or lemon when Alex strides into the room. He laughs at my expression, and sits on the side of the bed, fully dressed in a pristine, navy–blue suit that's molded to his to–die–for frame that I know is hiding underneath. It doesn't seem right that he's wearing clothes again, all buttoned up to perfection, while I'm wriggling under his duvet, naked.

"Morning, gorgeous." He leans in and slides an errant lock of hair behind my ear. His fingertips grazing my skin are enough to make my nipples perk up, and I squeeze my thighs together to ease the tension building there. I still can't believe I shared a bed with him and did all those things. And that it felt so good. I'm so freaking happy there are dance tunes blaring over everything going on in my head.

"Mm, thank you." I sit up straighter and let out a long, contented sigh. "Been up long?"

"Not long. But I'm late for the office."

I wish I could have woken up earlier and enjoyed the feeling of basking in his arms, but my comatose slumber prevented that luxury.

"Here, I got you a new phone." He places a spanking new device into my hand.

I rub sleep out of my eyes and stare at the sleek, white device. "You shouldn't have."

"Yes, I should. I need to be able to contact you."

I finger the *on* button and watch the screen come to life. "I can't accept this."

"Hayley, see it as your work phone that your employer is giving you."

I sit up straighter. "You were serious about that?" Excitement ripples through me at the thought of taking control of that gallery downstairs. Mixed in with the lust for this incredible man, I'm trembling at the sheer abundance of my luck.

"Are you okay?" he asks.

Like a maniac, I smile into empty space. Then, it hits me. All of it.

"Oh no! My flight! Dad thinks I'm coming home today! Alex ... I can't stay till September. That's ridiculous. What was I thinking? This is impossible." I lift the heavy tray off my lap, maneuvering it carefully on to the duvet, and slide off the bed, not caring that I'm naked. I scramble to the chair where clothes are lying in a heap. But they're all his clothes.

"Shit, Alex, where are my clothes?" I do a madwoman dance in front of the chair.

"Where you left them. In the gallery."

"Come on," I insist. I race over to the faded grandfather clock on his wall to check the time. "Jesus, seven ten."

"Hayley." Alex is standing before me, looking bemused.

"What, exactly, are you doing?"

I swat strands of hair from my face and search around for something to tie it back with. "What does it look like? I need to go."

"But—go where?" He reaches out to me. "We talked about this yesterday. I asked you to stay."

"Yes, but I thought ... I thought it was just ... you know ... talk." I redden. I may as well admit that I'd have said anything to have him do the things he did to me. "I didn't think you meant it *that* way."

He frowns. "Well, what other way is there?"

I stop moving. His unguarded expression of sheer incomprehension makes *him* seem naked to *me* for the first time.

I gulp and meet his gaze. "You mean— You want me to stay?"

Alex lets out a sigh. "Hayley, if you want me to say it again, I will."

As the truth of his words sink it, I need to slump back down on the bed. It's crazy. Dad will have a heart attack. And Uncle Stig's running around somewhere, God knows where. Or dead. I was so ready to leave this country. Until now.

Alex sits down beside me, his warmth seeping through my side. He pulls the top blanket up around my shoulders as I'm starting to shiver. "I want you to stay, but if you feel you can't, I won't pressure you." His fingers trail down my forearm, making the hairs spring up.

I clutch the blanket and pull both sides together at my chest. Call me a prude, but I can't talk career moves with my tits on display. "But how would that even work? I mean, in theory, if I were to stay?"

"I would get papers drawn up to employ you as a student worker. A decent wage. If, that is, you still feel you can make a go of this gallery idea? You'd have the creative freedom to set up the gallery for public viewing as you see fit. And you could stay in my room, if you want." Alex gestures to me and him with a vague, circular motion of his fingers.

I imitate his vague, circular gesture. "Another perk of the job, huh?"

He smiles broadly. "Every night. Every morning, too, if you wish."

"Plus breakfast in bed?" I'm smiling now. He makes it all sound so easy. But most importantly, he's couched it in terms that shows respect for me and who I am.

"Oh yes. Absolutely."

Christ, what do I have to go back to? Two months of summertime boredom while I wait for the semester to start. Besides, Alex is offering me a legitimate reason to stay. I'll be able to earn my own fare back to Portland and not rely on my flaky uncle. It's actually a no–brainer. "I have to talk to Dad first."

"Of course." He slaps his knees and rises. "I'll go and fetch clothes from your room. In the meantime, wear this." He hands me a gray terry cloth bathrobe. It's got the family crest on the pocket.

"I'm impressed," I say, running my fingers over the embroidered crest of two lions fighting. "Are there slippers to match?"

"I'll put it on the list of employee demands."

After Alex has delivered my clothes and gone again, I get dressed and carry the cup of tea down to my own bedroom. I start up Skype. It's 7:30 a.m. in England, 11:30 p.m. in Oregon. Mara's a night owl, so there's no danger she'll be in bed yet. And it's no surprise that she's still at work when I make contact. She seems to be slaving over architectural design details that her boss will probably never give her credit for.

"Are you out of your mind?" is her first response to my news that I'm staying in Fernborough for the rest of the summer.

"It's a once–in–a–lifetime opportunity," I say defensively.

"I'm sure it is. But. Well. Wow."

"Right?" A traitorous smile breaks out on my face.

She slaps her hand to her mouth. "No, don't tell me. You

and Big Cucumber?"

"Alex. His name's Alex."

"So, was he big, I mean, good?"

"Out of this world, Mara. I'm one part intoxicated, another part terrified, or something. I hardly know!"

"Okay, calm down."

"I'm fine." I laugh. "I'm great. I've never felt better. Oh, if only you were here, then it would be perfect."

"Seriously, Hayley. You need to think. Call your father. Tell him something. I saw him in Freddy's again this morning. I actually hid behind the shelves to avoid having *that* conversation with him. You. Need. To. Talk. To him."

Mara has always had a soft spot for my dad. Probably because her own father is a horrible narcissist and she spent more hours of her childhood and adolescence with us than in her own house. Her disapproval acts as a barometer of how well—or badly—I'm fulfilling my daughterly role. "I know," I wail. "He thought I was coming home today."

"Do it. Or he'll be catching a plane out there. You know he will."

After the call with Mara, I run all the arguments through my head again. It all sounds good. But is it good enough to withstand the guilt fest that's awaiting me when I lay it all out for Dad?

"Hayley!" Dad's face absolutely confirms my deepest fears. The lines of fatigue and anxiety around his eyes seem to have deepened.

"Are you all right, Dad?"

"I am now."

"Have you heard anything from Stig?"

I need to know what bullshit Uncle's been feeding him, if any.

Dad frowns. "Shouldn't I be asking you that? Last I heard was three days ago."

"Okay, well maybe he's going to contact you at some stage and explain where he's at, but the point is, he's not here with me, and I don't know what he's up to. But never mind that.

Dad ... I've decided to stay on here in Belgrave Castle for a few more weeks."

Sheer incomprehension washes over his face. "What do you mean? Your flight's tomorrow!"

Poor Dad. At this moment, I feel evil for disappointing him. "Yeah, I'm cancelling that. Or postponing, if the airline lets me."

"Until when?"

"Absolute latest before the start of the semester for sure." I suck in a breath. "The thing is, I've been very kindly offered a job in the family gallery here. It'll look great on my resume. It's almost impossible to get relevant work experience in the fine arts, and this'll really help. I'm staying here for two months maybe."

While he's still digesting my announcement, I add for good measure, "I'm fine, Dad."

"Are you? First you tell me Stig's in trouble and that you need to fly home right away, but then it's suddenly not a problem, he's disappeared, and you've decided to hang around there for two months because of some ... job. What am I supposed to think, Hayley?"

"That I'm in the right place at the right time, Dad."

"I'm not convinced. I'll fly over to you."

"No, Dad! Let me do this. I'm not a child anymore," I blurt.

I didn't mean to say it, but there *is* no other way to stop him taking matters into his own hands. "Don't waste money like that," I add in a softer voice. "We'll stay in touch by Skype. I promise."

He sighs, eyes forlorn. But there's still that knife I need to twist in his wound. My stomach tightens knowing that we're at a massive "before" and "after" threshold. After this point, he's never going to have the same level of respect for me— his darling daughter, his only child. Another brick of my pedestal is about to be cruelly wrenched away.

"There's another thing, Dad. I don't know how much you look at YouTube these days, but I think you need to see something, because you're going to hear it out of context from someone else for sure."

"What?" he says warily.

"It's just ... a sort of misunderstanding I was having in a nightclub with the duke." I chuckle nervously. "It's kind of how we met, I suppose. He'd insulted Uncle Stig. No big deal, but you know how it is with social media—they blew it way out of proportion. I'm sending you the links. Just look at it later, Dad. Tomorrow morning, not now."

When he clicks off, my heart's in tatters. I wanted to comfort him and to reassure him everything's going to be fine, but I've probably made him more miserable than he's been for a very long time.

# 18

ALEX

I am shocked by how much I wanted to stay with Hayley in bed all day. Normally, I can't get women out the door soon enough, but all I can think of is her smooth, golden skin and how to get my hands back on it the minute I break free from work this evening. I hope she doesn't back out. She's given me some indication of her father's protectiveness of her and I sense she's missing him.

I want to set things up for her properly, giving her access to all the galleries, and all of Father's dusty cabinets of artwork, and the freedom to work how she wishes. But, much trickier, I need to get ahold of her uncle and find out if he's bought off the Azerbaijanis or what the hell. Once that's sorted, I can concentrate on making Hayley's stay as perfect as possible and make the most of our time together.

Inside the tower, I grab an espresso from our little Nespresso machine and I approach the door of the conference room. Through the half–open door, I hear my siblings yapping animatedly. I pause at the threshold. They haven't seen me yet.

Ken is talking.

"The carrots and turnip crop yields are in serious danger of slipping. The Easton tenants are furious. Brexit is making everything impossible, and here we are, wasting hundreds of man hours on this dumb wedding. That prince is obviously only using us to get Abbeydale to lower their prices."

"Well, that's how tenders work," Letty replies.

"Yes, and we don't need them. It's just an ego trip for Alex."

I choose that moment to stride in.

Ken glances up at me, not a whit of embarrassment on his face. "And I reckon our chances are zero with the extra bad press we picked up. And when I say we, I mean you. Case in point, the last two YouTube scandals."

I scratch my jaw. "I'm working on getting those videos taken down. Or Marty is, anyway. He still needs to identify who put them up."

Letty pouts. "He's taking his time. I thought that spook could find out anything."

"Give him a break. He's MI6, foreign service, not MI5."

She blinks insolently. "I bet he's not really trying. Perhaps I should invite him here for brunch. Is he good looking?"

"No."

She pouts. "Maybe he can help us find Seb."

"He's already working on that," I snap.

"We need to think of some other way to get Seb back," Ken says.

"No." I slam my palm onto the table, making them both jump. "We need to win this Saudi wedding, people, please, concentrate!" I gulp back a familiar wave of agitation regarding Seb, but something about the feeling has changed. At first, I can't seem to identify what it is, what's causing this strange anger to bubble up inside of me.

But then it hits, like an ice–cold arrow. No longer am I annoyed that my older brother left me with all this responsibility and all this trouble that I never asked for.

Now, I'm annoyed I'll have to give it all up.

# 19

HAYLEY

There is no official job description, but that's the beauty of it. I've been in the gallery all day, dusting off the frames. Time is ticking by as it always does when I'm in a zone of creative thought. I'd move all the neo–Bauhaus paintings to the west wing and those Warholesque ones here nearer the entrance— he seems to have amassed a lot of those. I could design a snazzy entrance lobby by the door and a website to attract viewers and potential buyers, if the Belgraves are up for that. This collection seriously needs to be hauled kicking and screaming into the twenty–first century and the floors need a good scrubbing, too.

The more I burrow deeper into the task, the more my staying here makes a weird kind of cosmic sense. Mother would have been proud of me. It's exactly the kind of thing she'd have done.

But when the daylight fades, my confidence disintegrates. The only people happy with our arrangement are Alex and me, and maybe Letty. Not that anything has been explicitly stated, but at dinner an hour ago when Alex announced the idea, I got the vibe from the dowager duchess that I shouldn't be interfering in her late husband's things, or at the least that I'm wasting my time.

I need to get out of this room. I need to see Alex, wrap myself around his hard body, to feel what I felt yesterday at this time when everything felt wonderful. I need confirmation that I'm not crazy for hanging on here, and the only thing that will do that is Alex giving me a good mind–blowing fuck.

Back upstairs, I ask Mrs. B if she knows where Alex is as she passes by with a basketful of laundry. "I think he's down at the stables, dear."

I put on my coat and head down the flagstone path. Grasshoppers click in the grass and the dusk sky glows pink. From about a hundred feet away, I spot two figures—a man and a woman. The man is unmistakably Alex. Their conversation seems animated. I bash away a cloud of tiny flies and squint. It's not Letty with him. Someone smaller.

Oh no, the dowager duchess.

My first impulse is to turn and sneak back into the house. But it's too late—they've seen me because I swatted away those damn flies. I'm going to intrude if I progress further so I remain stupidly still, just standing there. I hear the name "Seb" being repeated. I know that's the brother who went on a holiday somewhere, but nobody talks about him. At least not when I'm around.

Well, now they know I'm here, so I may as well keep walking. When I reach them, their impassioned body language has normalized to stiff politeness and they're avoiding each other's eyes.

"Hey." Alex comes over and swings his arm around me. I slacken against his hard body. At least he's acting glad to see me, if not exactly naturally.

"I'll leave you to it," his mother says, tonelessly. She adjusts a winding plant on the trellis that was already perfectly arranged, and strides off, tugging her coat belt tighter around her trim waist. She looks great for someone in her late fifties, a graceful ager, like almost everyone in their circle.

Over her shoulder, she gives me a frosty once–over. Is this woman going to hate me forever?

"Everything okay?" he asks me.

"You tell me. Is your mother upset with you? Me? Us? Does she even know about us?"

"Yes, I told her."

"I'm sorry to cause you this trouble. If—"

"No." His arm tightens at my waist. "That's not it at all. There's ... so much you don't know. All that you see, and much more that you don't. And frankly, I'd rather you didn't."

I stare at him in confusion.

"In some ways, Belgrave Castle is a prison, Hayley. I have a love–hate relationship with it, if you will. Mother, she abhors the public and yet, we let them in thirty–odd days a year. One of those public days is coming up and she always gets angsty beforehand. My advice? Stay out of her way. I know I do."

"But, why do you need to open it up at all?"

He gives me a long, rueful look. "The eco–farming business isn't as profitable as we'd like. It's barely breaking even. Maintenance sucks up the budget like a ravenous monster. We have to plan carefully just to keep the roofs intact. Oh, we're crammed with antiques, you can see that, and paintings, but Mother plain rejects the idea of selling anything off, and especially the idea of anyone coming in and evaluating the worth of anything in the house. The only thing I have any control over is new business." He laughs a hollow laugh. "Sure you still want to be with me?"

"Of course, Alex," I half whisper. At this moment, the man standing before me is less the entitled, playboy duke that the media would have him be and more the head of family trying to make the balance sheets add up, just like everyone else. And I like him all the more for it.

He sighs. "My ideal solution is to go all out and win a splendiferous wedding. A Saudi royal wedding. It would set the precedent for similar high society weddings. You just need one reference like this and they'll come in droves. Five or six tightly controlled weddings would be far superior to letting the public ramble all over the property thirty times a year. But who cares what I think?"

After this surprising remark, he proceeds in a brisk walk through the rose garden and past the paddocks. I'm keeping up, but it's tough going in these useless sandals. He doesn't say anything, just swishes a stick back and forth, idly slashing at some high grass leaning into our path.

When he finally speaks again, his voice is tighter. "I promise. We'll all be able to relax a bit more when this Saudi wedding business is resolved one way or the other."

I study his worried face. "You *can* talk to me, Alex."

He stops walking and turns to me. "I know, but I think you've enough problems in your own family."

I grab his arm. "That doesn't stop me from caring what's going on with you."

"Oh, sweet Hayley." He tugs at the bow of my blouse until it unravels and his eyes, azure in the dusk, capture mine. There's an animal determination to his expression that finds a primal response in my body. A shiver of anticipation goes down my spine and nerve endings tingle all the way from my fingertips to deep between my legs. It's the moment I've yearned for all day and I'm already a goner. I shuffle closer to him.

## 20

ALEX

Hayley stands still for a second and then launches herself forward, grasping my shirt in her fist. I feel her pent–up energy. We crash together greedily, our mouths locking in a rough kiss. It's been too long since this morning.

She's tugging my shirt as she moves backward until she's up against the old beech tree. Through gritted teeth, she says, "Let's do it. Here. Now."

My cock springs to life and I peel the blouse away from her neck, covering her mouth and jaw with kisses that brand her mine, completely mine. Out here in the sunset, her hair burnished an intense copper, it's like the denouement of a cowboy film. Except this one is going to be X–Rated, if I have anything to do with it.

Luckily, we don't have any neighbors for miles around, because she's naked. I take one greedy look at her golden skin, the curves of her breasts, the waves of her hair draped artlessly over her collarbone. I place my hands on her hips. "Turn around," I say, gently maneuvering her.

With only a flicker of hesitation in her beautiful eyes, she complies. "Put your hands up against the tree," I whisper in her ear. Keeping my flat palm firm between her shoulder blades, I ease her forward. There's another moment of hesitation in her body but I keep the pressure on. "Trust me."

She leans forward, grasping the fat trunk of the tree with splayed fingers, letting out a giggle that turns into a sigh when I smooth my palm over the curve of her lower back. Then, as if to push me over the edge, she arches even more, her ass high in the air, creating an irresistible silhouette. Her concentrated silence and her rapid, shallow breathing tell me she wants this. I caress along her spine and down toward her crack until her gasping turn to moans, and she's trembling. I can't hold out much longer either.

I inch my palms over her buttocks, letting my fingers move slowly to her throbbing core. She's so wet already. When I make contact with her clit, she groans in relief, giving me a prelude to the ecstasy she'll be feeling soon.

"Oh God, Alex, please."

Her sweet moans turn my brain to mush. These condoms have been burning a hole in my trousers pockets all fucking day. I always have them with me now. Belt untied, pants falling, I free my cock, sheath it, position myself carefully at her soft, wet entrance. She nods, and I drive my hard length into her in one thrust. As we work up a rhythm—me thrusting, Hayley pushing back, gripping the knots in the bark as leverage, I reach around and clasp her mouth to muffle her groans of pleasure. She's trembling, sucking and biting down on my fingers. I pound faster until she goes over the edge, collapsing forward. I keep my grip on her hips as her moment of ecstasy draws out and I follow straight after, pouring everything I have into her.

# 21

HAYLEY

After a shattering orgasm, I come to, woozy. I'm leaning, spent, still gripping onto a tree so tight that the bark crumbles in my palm when the waves of pleasure finally recede to a level where I can think again. I suppose it's comical that I have a duke inside of me and we're gazing over a meadow where Gandalf and Frodo are looking curiously at us, the two naked humans doing something unspeakable up against their fence.

"Ah, look at them," I say.

"Don't worry, I've seen them do worse with the fillies on Gordon's farm." Alex drapes my shirt over my shoulders and leads me to the stables, the nearest building.

Sitting on the same bale of straw I sat on before with Letty, I shake the dust off my clothes and get dressed again, feeling scratches of straw remnants all over me. I can't believe how fast and furious that was. I couldn't have stopped it if I'd tried. And I'm not hurt, just a little raw, and pretty horny.

It only occurs to me when I'm fully dressed to check whether we were within view of the house and I peer out the stable window. To my relief, there's a huge wall and an orchard blocking the view.

"We're crazy," I say. "They could have seen us."

He comes over to sit on my bale of straw, kisses my forehead, my cheek, my neck. "God good, no. I was sure of that. I hope I wasn't too rough."

I shake my head.

He cocks an eyebrow. "Too gentle?"

I break into a smile. "Just right. Perfect."

"That's what they all say." He grins and leans back against a wall of straw, elbows crooked behind him, the picture of smugness.

I push his chest playfully and I'm silent, just letting the endorphins buzz around me in the dusk like the tiny dust flies. I wish I could capture this moment and bring it back home with me fully intact—the visuals, the smells, the sounds, and the amazing feelings.

"I told Dad," I say. "Told him I'm staying here for a while. For two months to be precise."

Alex sits forward, elbows on knees, and rubs his hands. "Yes, I was going to ask. So, is he okay with that?"

I shrug. "Could be better. But it's my life."

I'm doing my best to sound nonchalant. Alex has no idea how hard it is for me to leave Dad at home, worrying his head off, and how weird it feels to have weeks of this strange life of nobility ahead of me. At the same time, I don't want him to feel I don't appreciate the opportunity. And yet, I'd be lying to myself if I denied the real reason I'm here. And if that ever changes, it'll all come toppling down like a house of cards.

"He misses you," Alex says.

"Yeah." I slide into my jeans. "Let's get back to the house. Call me a princess, but I prefer satin sheets under me, not straw sticking into every goddamn orifice."

"I love it when you talk dirty." He brushes back my hair from my collarbone, pulls out a straw from my hair and blows it away. There's lust burning in his eyes and that's good because I'm ready to go again.

"So, how many times have you made love in a field?" I ask him, idly trailing my hand up his impressively hard thigh. It must come from swimming. I've never heard him mention any other kind of sport.

"Never."

"Okay, up against a tree then?"

"I've *fucked* against a tree before."

"Different tree?"

"Completely different tree." His gaze is unrelenting, its intensity pinning me back against the straw. "But never made love."

"Oh, there's a difference?"

"Yeah, there's a difference."

My heart's beating so hard, it pushes words out of my mouth. "Care to show me? But not in a field?"

His hand reaches out and he entwines his fingers in mine. Then he pulls me up to standing and draws me close into his beautiful, hard body. "It would be an honor."

## 22

ALEX

Hayley and I have been together five nights in a row, love–making, fucking, whatever you want to call it, because I no longer know the semantic difference. With her, it's all intense, dirty, fun, and fucking amazing.

Even with Ken needling me even more these days, Letty being meddlesome and Mother, tragic, nothing can get me down, because my spirits seem suspended in some strange post–coital heaven. I've never had a live–in lover before, maybe that's the difference. But something tells me it's not just that. After our sessions, I get this sense of peace with myself that no woman has ever given me before. Just that—a simple peace. Women normally make me nervous or flat–out bored by the second date, always putting me on my guard. But every time I wrap my arms around Hayley and breathe in her scent, it just gets better and better. Perhaps it's true that some people are just meant to be together.

Philistine that I am when it comes to art, she's teaching me. The details often go over my head—school of this, style of that, post–this and neo–that, I can't see much difference. It's comforting that somebody like her is looking after Father's legacy, and I love listening to her talk about the paintings like they're living entities with opinions of their own as to where they should be hung and whose company they should keep.

In a strange way, with Hayley so involved in his obsessive hobby, Father seems closer now. I wish she could have met him when he was alive. They'd have got on well. She'd have challenged his stubborn opinions on good taste, steered him away from the truly hopeless artists—I suspect there were plenty of those—and he'd have adored her for it.

During breaks in work, I go into the gallery and I always pick her up just before six so we can ... get dressed for dinner together.

Today, as she's sitting at the dressing table, brushing out her luxurious, chestnut hair, she's talking again about the collection of prints by a Welsh painter called Myles Lillienthal maybe being worth something. I think she means those canvasses with Jackson Pollack–like random splashes of paint. She's getting that same manic look in her eyes that Father used to adopt whenever he'd discovered someone "new."

"I researched him. He's already sold one for fifty thousand in the Philippines, and one is Paris for twice that. He's getting popular. Our specimens are much bigger though, and all done in his peak phase between 2000 and 2010. We just need to open the gallery up, spread the word, and bring in prospective buyers," she says. "They'll want to see it firsthand, not just internet photos."

"Sure it's not just a bunch of crap?" I'm wary of anything that'll make me look silly or pretentious.

She shakes her head firmly. "This is the real deal. We find the right buyer, I reckon it would solve your tax problem."

I look at her in surprise.

She bows her head. "Letty told me, Alex. About the looming tax bill being your immediate worry and that the farming accounts didn't add up this spring. Sorry. But this isn't just a quick fix, Alex. This could be a long–term plan." Her glowing hazel eyes, full of hope and tenderness, scan my face. My heart thumps out a record–breaking drum solo when I read between her lines. Never mind the money, is she actually thinking beyond September? Because I know I am, but I also know that the best way to send Hayley running is to suggest anything to her about how she should live her life.

"Long term ... sounds good," I say casually.

"Yes." She looks down and examines her fingernails. "It kinda does."

The bell chimes out six and we rise to go for dinner. I suspect she's as glad as I am for the interruption.

◆◆◆

"Care for a duel?" Ken asks as the puddings are cleared away.

My first reaction is to want to scream, "Hell, no!" in my best American accent. I want time with my woman. But when was the last time Ken asked me to do something with him after dinner, just for fun? Right. Never. Or not since Father died, anyway. So I agree and mutter to Hayley that I'll catch up with her later, but not too much later. I'm not quite sure I'm going to win this fencing bout, so I don't ask her to come watch. She seems happy enough to skip off to the living-room with Letty anyway.

"Is this your way of settling some argument?" I ask Ken as we stroll together to the hunting room where the fencing gear is stored. I'm still somewhat peeved as I take down my protective chest padding and blow off the dust. "If so, what did I do wrong?"

"No, you idiot. I need a few bouts of practice before my course starts up again in September."

"Are all your recreational activities combative?"

"It helps with the anxiety."

"I can think of other things." I flash him a grin.

He responds with a long–suffering look. "In my experience, that's combative too."

"Maybe you just haven't found the right one."

He cocks an eyebrow. "And I suppose you have?"

I slide on a glove. "Yes." Because there *is* no other way to say it. Why make up complications when there are none? Why downplay a feeling that's natural and glorious? The only problem Hayley and I have is that her life's in Oregon and mine is here and that the clock is ticking on us. Mercilessly.

"Are you actually serious? Alex. Think about this."

"I've done all the thinking on the subject that I need to."

He shakes his head. "It won't be easy on her, fitting in. And you're giving up your chances of marrying your way out of financial trouble."

I tighten the straps on my chest guard. "Jesus, Ken, were you always this romantic?"

"I'm just trying to help."

"I appreciate your concern, but focus on your own dating life. Or lack of it."

I'm all dressed but he's having problems putting on the protective jacket, which should be snug, but not this snug. "That used to fit you perfectly," I comment.

"Yeah." He tugs at the side zip, which is never going to get past his rib cage.

"If you'd stop all the boxing workouts and the protein shakes, you might have a chance. It's unnecessary."

"Damn it." He rips off the chest guard and hangs it back on the hook. "Problem solved. Can I trust you not to stab me in the heart?"

"Depends on how much you piss me off."

"Hey. I'm a worrier. That's what I do."

"I know."

We're finally ready to go, helmets and gloves are on, and we've drawn out lines in the clay beside the pear orchard. The ground is most level here and shaded from the wind by the high stone wall.

"En garde, prêt, allez," Ken says, in his phony French accent. He may be more mathematical than me, but linguistically, he's a disaster.

We parry. Our foils gleam and clink in the evening sun, scaring off the ravens from the surrounding oaks. Ken's lunges are impressive. Both of us are rusty on the footwork, neither of us particularly nimble, but at least we're even.

We're silent, both concentrating on not letting the other man score any points. Ken's as competitive as I am when it comes to sports. Of course, as soon as he's two points up, he decides it's time to chatter so he'll distract me and keep his lead. "Mother's driving herself to distraction about Seb."

"I know."

Ken backs up to the start position. "I told her to wait. But what else can we do?"

"Beats me," I say. I'm not being completely honest here. I could organize a search party the length and breadth of Britain if I really wanted to. I'd pull in favors from other members of the nobility. I'd persuade Marty to dig deeper. But these days, I'm only paying lip service to the whole idea of Seb returning. I've actually told Marty to call off the search and focus instead on Hayley's uncle. Yes, I want to know that Seb's safe, but if he doesn't want to come back, then maybe it's not quite the disaster I once thought. I'm perfectly prepared to leave it up to him.

"Maybe he's become a Buddhist monk," Ken says as he parries.

"Seb?"

He shrugs. "Anything's possible."

"In that case you're all stuck with me."

Ken stills for a moment. "You're not doing such a bad job, you know. "

My heart swells with this rare praise and I'm caught totally off guard when the tip of his foil presses into my chest protection, to the point of pain. Another win to him.

I can't see his expression through the grille of the mask. "Are you talking about fencing or being the duke?" I ask, just to be sure.

"The latter. Your fencing will always suck. But at least you made a serious indent on our email backlog and sorted out those grain prices. It feels like there's a boss in the office again. So, is it Hayley's influence?"

I lunge at him. "Are you kidding? She's driving me crazy."

He leaps backward over a gnarled tree root. I chase after him, laughing. We're out of bounds now, no longer following fencing rules. He's stronger than I am which is all the more reason not to let him think for one moment that he can beat me.

It turns into a swashbuckling replay of every sword fight we've seen in the movies, from Caribbean pirates to Jedi battles. We hum the theme tunes, tunelessly, but Letty's not around to scold us. This feels so great. So freeing.

Afterward, exhausted and sweaty, I whip off my helmet and throw my gloves inside. We sit on two tree stumps, gasping in the humid evening air, drinking cool water from the pump by the boathouse.

Ken doesn't seem to want to talk, so I begin. "Tell me, am I crazy? I want her to stay. Beyond the summer. I've a feeling this could work out."

Ken clenches his hands together and says nothing, just watches my face, so I continue. "With her attracting pundits to the gallery, perhaps even potential buyers for some of the lesser pieces." I wince, and wait for an explosion of argument but he's still silent.

"Even if hosting high–profile weddings doesn't pan out, I'm thinking we may have a viable business on our hands with a gallery like Hayley's planning it. I know it's a departure from the usual, but so what? It's good business and we may manage to cut down on the public days even more."

I look at him again, my chest tight with anxiety. I've laid it all out here, my gut feelings about how business could be run at Belgrave.

He throws me a look. "Sure it's not just your dick overruling your brain?"

"I'm not sure of anything," I retort. *Except that I want her to stay.*

My brother says nothing for a full minute. Then he tilts his head slowly side to side. "Alex, she's got a whole life over there. She's up against all hell here. Does she even know the extent of it?"

"But you're not opposed, per se?" I hate that I'm begging for acceptance for someone three years younger than I am whose disposable income from Father's will gets swallowed up periodically at the horse races.

He throws up his hands. "Who cares what I think anyway?" He catches my earnest gaze. "It's Mother you have to worry about."

# 23

HAYLEY

While Alex is fencing with Ken, I head toward the living room, hoping for a view of them out the bay window, but the room is occupied by Letty and her piano tutor. I'm not in the mood for music. I glide past, aiming for the library. I stop at the second floor, Alex's room. Well, *our* room now, I suppose.

Inside, I linger by the window, relishing how the Belgrave estate stretches in all four directions, offering majestic views as far as the eye can see. It's amazing how quickly you get used to living in exalted circumstances. I'm going to miss all this when I leave.

*When I leave.* I quash that thought. We've only just started. I need so much more time to understand how this place works, how this society works and to find my little niche in it without stepping on anyone's toes.

I step back and bump into something. I look down at the mahogany writing desk. There's an array of office utensils neatly laid out, that beautiful Cartier pen I saw on day one, and a whole set to match. I run my fingers lovingly over them. It's the kind of table where, in an age gone by, a man would sit down to write a beautiful love letter to his lady. I toy with the idea of writing Alex a little love note and leaving it on his pillow. Something funny and obscene.

The coaster that I first wrote my name and number on is there on top of the little cupboard built into the desk. My heart glows as I lift it, the memories of *Jayvee's* flooding back, my awestruck first impression of Alex, the utter confusion that followed, the first time I saw him standing outside the main door of Belgrave Castle. Our wild goose chase to find Uncle Stig in a bowling alley.

Sitting down on the worn leather chair, I pick up the pen and pull out a blank sheet of paper and start doodling. First I draw the beautiful clock perched in the middle of the table. My swinging legs kick against something hard under the table that wasn't there the last time I sat here. I look down. It's a black briefcase with brass clasps. I look at it, think, no, and keep doodling. After five minutes, the fruit of my labor is a sketch of a suitcase with an explosion of fireworks, twirls, and question marks coming out of it. The universe is trying to tell me something.

So I bend down, sighing at my own curiosity, pull out the briefcase and click the clasps, fully expecting it to be locked. But it opens. There's a stack of A4-sized papers, all uniform. Tenants' accounts, I'm guessing. Alex must have brought work back to the bedroom for once. But then the name on the cover of one dossier catches my eye. "Stig Lawson." I frown, and dip my head closer. Did I read that right? He's got a *file* on Uncle Stig? The next one causes me to cry out loud into the room. "Hayley Cochrane." And yet another: "David Cochrane."

I grow cold. My skin tingles all over. Bad enough me … but *Dad?* What could this mean? I glance over to the door, which is closed. With quivering fingers, I lift my own folder up.

The MI6 stamp on the top left looks official, not that I've ever seen one before. Frantically, I flick through the dozen or so pages. It's roughly printed black and white document with hurried looking date stamps in the upper left corners of each page. There's a list of "sightings"—terse accounts of my whereabouts in London since I arrived in the country. Along with that, a background history—my schools, grades even. A grainy photo taken from my blog. The details of my flight from Portland. And the one I'd booked but cancelled. I gasp.

What is he *doing* with this?

Next up is Dad's. My blood runs cold with fury. He's an innocent man who has nothing to do with anything and he's never even set foot in this country. What *is* this? Is it even legal?

Dad's file lists the stuff I know. The date of my birth. Mom's death. There's a passage on Mom, her father, the location of her gallery. Then a further couple pages about her father, my grandad, his famous newspaper business. There are some articles about misdeeds committed in order to bolster the business—extortion, blackmail.

I slam the report shut. I'm so mad, I could rip these documents to shreds, kick over this table, set the place on fire. I need to do something. Preferably something destructive.

But I won't. Because then I wouldn't find out *why*. I need to know, and for that, I must stay calm even if it kills me.

♦ ♦ ♦

What seems like hours later, but only registers twenty minutes on the clock, I hear his footsteps in the corridor, slower than normal, as though he's tired. I bolt upright on the chair where I'd been simmering in anger. Seconds later, the door opens. Alex takes a step in and then rears back when he sees me.

"My darling, am I glad to see you." He strides toward me.

But my heart is made of stone. "Don't you 'my darling' me. What is this?" I jerk my thumb at the files open on the desk.

He looks down. It doesn't seem to register with him for a moment, but then he winces. "Oh."

"What's this about, Alex?"

"They're nothing. A routine check, that's all. I've a friend—"

"Routine?" I laugh bitterly. "What were you looking for? Criminal charges? Evidence of STDs?"

"If you'd let me explain."

I rise from the chair, pick up a folder and slap it back down on the table for emphasis. "Believe it or not, we're innocent."

"But of course you are."

I ignore him. "You have nothing on my uncle either, so don't bother trying to insinuate that. Nothing that compares to what we have on you. Possession of classified documents? Spying on me? I should report you. Something tells me it wouldn't go in my favor. I demand to know why."

"Hayley, I know it's unpleasant for you to see this." He takes another step closer and I back off, toward the window.

"No, Alex. I need an explanation. Give me something."

"Fine." He holds up a palm toward me. "I owe you that." He flops down on the bed but I remain where I am, standing by the table with my back to the window.

"You know we're bidding for the Saudi wedding, right?"

I half turn. "Uh–huh."

"Well, the prince's aides are extremely fussy about security. They wish to know the identity and history of anyone resident here and ensure there are no connections to anyone who might be plotting to kill him, and by all accounts there are enough of those, from Taliban officials to members of his immediate family. Unless we comply with their every desire, we don't have a hope of beating the competition who will no doubt provide all they're asking for and more."

"Oh please," I scoff. "You expect me to believe that?"

A flash of hurt crosses his face but I'm too far gone to care. "Yes, actually," he says.

"Well, that's very convenient, isn't it, just like everything else in your life. How manipulative, Alex, keeping everything on a need–to–know basis."

His jaw clenches. "Not manipulative. Protective. Remember *you* came to *me* crying for help."

"Because you got us in the mess in the first place with

your crazy attempts to get on the front pages! Yes, Alex. So how does ruining Uncle's reputation, and mine, fit in with your desire to appear squeaky clean to the Saudi princes of this world, tell me that?"

He takes a step closer. For a moment, I wonder if I'm going to weaken and let him smooth talk his way out of it, because he probably could if he reached out and touched me.

Alex spreads his arms. "I admit it, the YouTube thing was unfortunate. And I need to explain all that to you … someday. But Hayley, your uncle was in deep shit, with or without my help. I needed to know what I was letting myself in for, having you here. Hence the files."

I laugh hoarsely. "In case what? I try to assassinate the prince? Or maybe you just don't trust me around your paintings and needed to check up I wasn't some kind of criminal like you're convinced my uncle is."

His mouth flattens. "Nice theory, Hayley. Except do you really think I'd give you the keys to the gallery if I thought you were a thief?"

The logic of this hits me hard but my temper flares way out of control. "But still you think you need to dig out my family records and display them to this prince. Is this what you do to all riff–raff who enter your palace? Oh, I know, it doesn't matter about my privacy because I'm just a commoner."

Alex struts around me in a wide circle, shaking his head. "You want to know about privacy, well, how about this?" He yanks out his phone and points to it. "Every move I've ever made is common knowledge. You're worried about one YouTube video? Try a hundred. And the prince has records on our family dating back to the sixteenth century. He doesn't just know what I had for breakfast, he knows what my great–great–great–great–grandfather had for breakfast in bloody 1702."

I'm stunned, more at the fact that he's so agitated than anything he's saying. I watch the lines of agitation on his forehead increase and then recede. .

"Yes, and this is why Seb would never let anyone stay in the house. Ever. But that's his approach. I'm doing it my way. If that means extra measures, it's my responsibility and I do take it seriously. Even if—" he looks at me sternly. "I'm not as good at subterfuge as Seb is. Anyone snooping around will find out what they want."

"Seb? Why the hell are you talking about *Seb?*" I'm yelling to cover my own feeling of guilt, because, yes, I was snooping.

Alex snaps his gaze away. "Forget about him." After a long, terrible silence, he adds in a much softer tone, "Don't do this. Give me a chance, Hayley. Please. Give us a chance."

He reaches out, beseeching. His need is raw and genuine. He's never played games in the way he uses words. He's never tried to manipulate my feelings or hide his own. That means so much to me, regardless of the stuff he does behind my back.

I'm melting into a puddle of goo, almost buying the story about the Saudi prince's need for security. It stings like hell, but if it's the price to pay to be with this man, then I'll pay it. I'm not someone who does the silent treatment thing when it goes against my deeper wishes.

"I got a shock," I say in a conciliatory voice.

"I should have told you." He caresses my cheek. "I apologize. I've been running around like a madman recently, and I didn't see it through your eyes and of course it was deplorable of me. In the future, I'll share everything I get from my source with you. That's a promise."

"There's going to be more? Sounds like I'll have to behave myself," I say, still shaken at the idea that Alex really does have spies working for him.

His eyes glow in the low evening light. "No. Nobody's tracing you anymore...except me." His hands snake around my waist and pull me into his hard body. I mold myself against him, hungry for him. Sliding his fingers up under my T–shirt, he cups his hands over my bare breasts, trapping my nipples tight between his fingers. Breathing against my stretched neck, he murmurs, "Forgiven?"

I nod. Because he is.

## 24

ALEX

I may look composed as I sit here with Ken and Letty in the conference room, but I've got the jitters. The teleconference with Prince Al Faisal bin Oman starts in five minutes.

I'm wearing my trusty chalk–stripe suit from Gieves & Hawkes. Hayley had fun helping me get dressed this morning. She couldn't believe how many silk ties I owned, and I couldn't believe how fantastic they looked on her when she tried each of them on her naked body. She said the navy blue and silver one brought out my eyes best and made me look serious, so I took her word for it, and then I used the tie to ... enhance our morning routine.

"Is it okay to show some skin?" Letty asks, waking me from my dirty thoughts.

"What?"

"Some skin. Is this prudish enough?" She's tugging at the lace trim of her dress sleeve.

"The prince doesn't expect western women to defer to his country's dress code any more than he expects me to drag out the cloak and coronet. Just relax, you're fine. We've every chance of winning this," I tell her in my most assured tone. "I'm going to conduct the intro in Arabic. He'll appreciate that."

"But his English is perfect. He went to that private school in Geneva," Letty says.

"It's only polite to try." I turn the laptop camera on and check the visuals. We're seated so I'm in the middle and my siblings to either side of me, Father's portrait looming overhead. Lighting is perfect. The microphone is picking up everything clearly. We're all set.

As the video link is made, we adjust our postures and smile into the camera. The prince and entourage are seated at a large oval table, surrounded by gold and cream decor and fresh white lilies in huge white vases. "Good morning, Prince Faisal," I say in Arabic to the assembly of white–robed men—and one veiled woman.

The prince's eyes gleam in surprise at my greeting. Nods all around. I'm guessing the old fogies over in Abbeydale can't even pronounce the Prince's name correctly.

"How long have you been learning Arabic, Your Grace?" an aide to the right of the prince asks in Arabic. I'm gratified that he's using my title. Of course I should expect no less from any aide of this very well–read, cosmopolitan prince.

"A few weeks."

"Impressive." He gives a tiny nod. "I am the interpreter, in case I am needed."

"Thank you." I consider the ice broken, and I settle back a fraction on my chair, giving Letty a covert wink.

"We appreciate all the effort you have put into your application," the aide to the left of the prince says, in only slightly accented English. "And for full compliance with our deadlines and preferences. As you are aware, His Highness desires a low–key wedding."

*"Inta mithlayy,"* I say, looking directly at the prince. *You're like me.* For my own pride, if nothing else, I need to engage the top man in the conversation and not just let his aides do all the talking.

A quick frown crosses the prince's smooth brow. His whole party goes deathly still. His Highness turns to his interpreter who leans in and speaks in low tone.

"What'd I say?" I mumble to Ken and Letty.

The consternation continues on the other side. Finally, the interpreter straightens and produces a forced smile. "Did you, Your Grace, mean, perhaps, to say, *inta mithli?* 'You're like me?'"

"Uh, yes. That's what I said."

The interpreter slowly shakes his head. "No, you said *inti mithlayy* with a *shaddah* on the final syllable."

"I did? Does that mean something else?"

"It means, 'You're gay.'"

I sink my head in my hands. Letty and Ken inhale sharply.

My head's spinning when I look up again. "My sincere apologies, Your Highness."

There is some more murmuring. More heads bent. The Prince waves off his interpreter and says in crystal, sharp International Boarding School English. "I think it might be better if we proceed in English."

"Yes, Your Highness, of course."

There's a twinkle in his eyes, but whether it's because he's got a sense of humor or he's envisioning my death by stoning in his local town square, I can't tell. "Yes, my dear cousin, I attended boarding school in Switzerland for four years where I learned French and English. It is rusty, as they say. However, I will endeavor to avoid any errors."

He's using "cousin," a term that the British Royalty use toward a duke. Ironic humor, perhaps. And he's smiling again. "You have a most beautiful home. Tasteful and secluded. I do, however, have concerns regarding publicity and security."

He pauses for dramatic effect. I let the moment stretch out. Only a fool would jump in now and offer information.

"My advisers have also called attention to some of your activities on social media, my dear duke. I hope you are not planning on insulting me publicly like you did your unfortunate US ambassador?"

Again, I can't tell whether he's joking or not. "That was a misunderstanding, Your Highness. We're all friends now."

SARA FORBES

"Good. I also understand your brother has managed the estate until recently? All business matters of import?"

*Damn* those Saudi intelligence agencies. I nod in resignation. I've no idea where this is going and I just want him to get to the point. Have we won or not?

"So why is he not at this meeting?"

I pause. "Following the death of my father, I have chosen to take the reins, Your Highness."

The prince turns and mumbles to his advisers on his left.

"I must inform you that we have chosen to do the wedding at Abbeydale."

My stomach plummets. We all sink back into our chairs. Then anger bubbles to the surface. He'd already decided and just wanted to show how much info he'd unearthed about Seb. Why? Power?

"Please do not take it so harshly. I decided with my advisors some days ago after weighing up all the options. It was a difficult decision. However, the reason I insisted on this face to face meeting is another matter."

"I'm all ears, Your Highness." I'm utterly unable to keep bitterness out of my voice now and I don't even try.

"My esteemed cousin, I hear you are a pilot, yes?"

"I can fly small planes or a helicopter, yes."

"We require a fast, comfortable, reliable and utterly discreet transportation from Kent to Oxford. It is extraordinarily difficult to arrange with local services. Therefore, I am appealing to you."

"You want me to give you a ride?"

"I will reimburse you for your trouble."

"No trouble. No reimbursement required," I say automatically. "It would be my pleasure."

There's a flurry of confusion and discussion. Finally, the prince turns to me. "Would one hundred thousand pounds cover it?"

My eyebrows shoot up. "It might, if we ran the thing on Dom Pérignon."

The prince offers a polite smile and then looks me directly

140

in the eyes. Even though digital media I feel the weight of his authority. "I'm paying for the discretion, not the fuel. Please accept, or I shall be obliged to take my business elsewhere."

"You've got a deal," I say quickly.

After the call, we sit in stunned silence, Letty, Ken and I.

"Well," Ken says.

"I'm sorry," I say, unhooking the webcam. "I was so sure we'd pull this wedding off and start a snowball effect. For now, it's back to the drawing board."

"But the consolation prize is shiny," Letty says.

"And with no effort hardly at all." Ken pats my arm. "Gives you an excuse to get up there again, no?"

I shrug. "Yeah. Shame not to do it. Seems to be all I'm good at."

That night, I discuss it with Hayley. It's the first night since we've been together that I don't want to jump her bones. I feel so defeated.. "I just thought it was going somewhere. You know, a new start in a way. Something that was *mine* ... something that wasn't ... Seb's." I sink back against the pillows.

She slides her hand up and down my shoulder, perfectly sympathetic, but I wonder if she really understands the significance of this. And I wonder if the Saudi wedding bid symbolizes my dukedom in a way—a high profile shot in the dark that didn't quite work out. Now I have to face up to reality and trudge my way through Seb's business again. I have to show Hayley I'm the man she thinks I am.

"Hey," Hayley's voice is soft and seductive. "Don't give up just because the first one doesn't work out. The next bid will be easier, I guarantee you. "

I clasp her hand in mine and press it to my heart. "Don't worry, Darling. It'll all look brighter in the morning."

## 25

ALEX

We are well into harvest season and a cool breeze wafts across the castle grounds from the east. It's been two weeks since the call with the prince. I won't lie and say it still doesn't sting, but I'm focusing now on my new reality—harvesting plans, quotas, fertilizer procurement for autumn, crop rotation planning for next year. Settling squabbles between tenants is another task I was previously unaware of, but I actually enjoy that bit. It's a lot to do, and I know I'm still not completely on top of it, but I'm getting there.

Hayley's uncle has popped up in the news, but only way down the agenda, almost invisible against the furor of what's happening in the government. He seems to be back doing his normal job as ambassador after his purported "break for health reasons". I suspect Marty has instructed him not to contact us because Hayley hasn't heard from him. I can't say I'm devastated. Marty says he doesn't know the details but confirmed that the danger has passed for sure, and that if I wanted to buy stocks in a certain oil company, he could probably give me a recommendation. Both he and I are happy to close that chapter. I burnt the files on Hayley and her family.

Our next open house day is tomorrow and Ken, Letty and

I are going over the last-minute logistics. I truly don't care if the lace place–mats cost £2.99 or £3.99 and frankly, I doubt I ever will. I don't have time for this. My siblings have been a great help though, taking over most of the work on that front while I concentrate on the farms.

Meanwhile, Hayley has cleared out the west wing section of the gallery and made it public ready. She's only had a shoe-string budget—from my own savings—but the floors have a new coat of varnish and new curtains have been draped of rich cherry red. It looks superb. And Hayley looks so happy, so fulfilled. She even admitted to enjoying this aspect of the art world more than being an artist cooped up in an attic.

I'm keeping our gallery experiment extremely low key for Mother's sake. She's still queasy about letting the *hoi polloi* anywhere near Father's "dungeons" as she calls them. So, the gallery is just a whisper of a suggestion on the bottom of the sign in the ticket kiosk, like a coy afterthought. But I know from experience that some people are very good at reading fine print and that news will travel by word of mouth if the pioneering visitors like what they see.

"I don't know whether it's the public she dislikes most or the fact that it's my idea," Hayley grumbles as I visit her at lunchtime with a basket of goodies I nabbed from the kitchen on my way down. Her tender face is all scrunched up with worry. My patience with Mother for continuing to act frostily toward her is wearing thin. Especially as September is looming, and the start of Hayley's term is just two weeks away, so I need desperately to come up with a plan. And it would help if everybody at Belgrave Castle were to be more than welcoming towards my girlfriend.

"Mother has no say in it." I lean in and kiss her. "Or this."

She grins into the kiss and I'm heartened to see her looking more cheerful. We're kissing and hip grinding our way down the corridor so we can eat in the sunny alcove at the end when we see Ken ahead, so we detach from each other.

"Alex, just coming to get you," he says, voice sharp.

"Someone drove into the private car park. I don't recognize them but maybe you do."

"I'll check it out." I turn to Hayley. "I'll be back in a minute, sweetheart. Just work away on the sandwiches yourself. They're your favorite."

When I get outside, there's a maroon Mercedes squatting at the end of the family driveway. Nobody I recognize. How dare they park there? If it's a limousine service, I'll put them right out of business.

Ken slides up beside me. "Is George off sick, or what? He should have stopped them."

"Not that I know of."

He grabs my arm. "Alex, don't do anything rash."

I shake him off and scuttle down the steps. I've no patience with trespassers. But as I stride across the gravel toward the car, I get this buzzing in my head. An awareness, a sixth sense. This is no limousine service. I'm supposed to *know* who this is.

A tall, tousle–haired figure in a black shirt and black jeans emerges from the driver seat and confirms what my heart already suspected.

Seb.

At first my legs won't move. I just stare while the waves of incomprehension wash over me. I didn't expect this. A part of me must have decided he was dead, or if not clinically dead, then so furious with the situation that he considered us dead to him. I falter, stumble, and then run toward my older brother. We embrace tightly.

"Seb?" I'm laughing, panting, fighting for words. "What the hell?"

He pushes me back. He looks grave, but otherwise healthy. His hair's messier than I remember it, tumbling down over his forehead to meet his dark brows and eyes. He'd look relaxed if it wasn't for his perpetual expression of misgiving. He's wearing black, his favorite color.

"Where the hell have you been?" I ask.

He turns to Ken, who's just run up, and embraces him

too. We stand as a trio of brothers for the first time in two months. It feels incredible, but disorienting.

"You join a cult or something? I mean, look at you." I pause to wait for his answer as you have to do with Seb, if you want any answer at all.

"I stayed with friends for a while," Seb says vaguely.

A million new questions roar up in my mind, but duty dictates they wait. "Quick, we must tell Mother. And Letty. They'll be over the moon. Come on." I'm attempting to drag a hundred–and–eighty–pound man toward the castle entrance but he's not budging an inch.

"Mother already knows," Seb says quietly.

My hands slacken and drop away from him. "Oh."

"I told her I was coming home," Seb says.

So I'm the last the know. Well, Ken too, and Letty.

"Good," I say, trying to keep my tone light. "This is where you belong."

Something like hurt flashes in his eyes. "Are you sure?"

My answer doesn't shoot out straight away, as, perhaps, it should. If he'd asked me this a month ago, perhaps just a week ago, I'd have yelled yes. Haven't I been pleading with the gods to bring him back home? My plan was to bear the title but let Seb run the show. The whole thing. And it was a good plan. Win–win, or so I'd thought. Until it changed. Until shouldering responsibility and helping people wasn't the living nightmare I thought it was, but rather something … bigger than I am. Something worth doing.

The *only* thing worth doing.

I'm clinging onto the hope that he doesn't want the responsibility back. That he's found some other life somewhere in the world and is just testing me. And that, too, would be very Seb–like. We stroll toward the castle in silence.

Finally at the base of the steps, he runs his hand over his jaw and breaks the long silence.

"Alex, Mother told me things. All I had to do was log on to the Internet to see the damage. I couldn't sit there and let Mother suffer in silence. That is why I came back."

"It hasn't been *all* negative."

"I've heard otherwise. This Saudi wedding?"

"We need the business."

"We have a business. That was a gamble. A reckless one at that."

"Which could have worked." I feel myself slipping into my old pattern with him. Him on the attack, me on the defense. Seb the sensible, Alex the joker.

Seb shakes his head. "See? There can't be two chefs running the kitchen."

"I agree."

His gaze wanders over my face. My quick affirmation surprised him. Then he focuses downward, kicks at the ground, scattering gravel. "Look, if you actually want this job—"

"No, Seb. You've wanted this job for as long as you've been alive. You've lived it. You deserve it."

"It's not what Father wanted."

I wince. It was what Father wanted until the media forced his hand by exposing Seb. "Your place is here, head of the family business, head of the family. It always has been and it always will be as long as you're alive."

"Alex—"

"No, hear me out. I understand why you ran away, but now that you're back we can get the business back to the way it was—with you as the boss. I just kept the seat warm for you. We're all behind you, one hundred percent."

I glance to Ken for confirmation. For a split second, he looks bewildered, but then nods, just in time.

"You'd go against Father's wishes then," Seb says.

I fold my arms. I'm kind of losing patience. "He's dead. In case you hadn't noticed. Take your place as director back, please."

Seb cocks his head and gives me an appraising look. "Shake on it?"

I look down at his outstretched hand. This isn't want I want. Not at all. But it's the right thing to do, by Seb, and by my family. They expect it.

But something collapses inside as I take his cool, long–fingered hand in mine. I'm giving away something I built up together with Hayley—a foundation for our future. For the first time in my life, I've felt it's enough to be me. She's never questioned my place at the head of the family. To her, it wasn't weird at all, but the natural order of things. And I acted accordingly. Now she's going to think I pulled the wool over her eyes. And, in a way, I did.

It feels like the handshake of death. And yet, if I refused my brother, I'd hate myself. In our family, a handshake between siblings means sealed and done forevermore. No legalese required. We will formalize all this with the lawyers later, but we don't need to.

"Your Grace," he says. It's the first time he's addressed me like this, and it makes my skin crawl.

"Fuck off," I say.

I wander up to the castle, not feeling half as ducal as I did this morning. Freedom doesn't taste as good as it should. At least I'll have more time for the one person who still believes in me.

## 26

HAYLEY

I'm in my own little world in the gallery. Alex never came back for lunch, so I gobbled up his turkey and lettuce sandwiches. This is hungry work. I'm just finished polishing the frame of the Julie Dufor still life when there's a rap on the door. I leap up.

I open the door with a sly grin. But it's not Alex, it's Letty.

She flounces into the room in her fake fur vest, billowing silk blouse and gypsy skirt. "Hayley, oh, I'm glad I found you, it's all such a commotion and ... oh!" She does a twirl in the center of the room. "Oh, I like what you've done with the place. So this is what you two have been busy with down here."

"Thanks." I steer her in the direction of the highlights, starting with the Lillienthal collection in the back room. Soon she gravitates toward the faux–rococos as I knew she would, as surely as Alex went for the neo–Bauhaus. I enjoy the rapt look on her face as she does the rounds.

"But what did you come down to tell me, Letty?"

"Oh." Her hand flies to her mouth. "Would you believe, I actually forgot for a moment. Seb's back."

"Seb? Your brother Seb?"

"Yes, Seb. Seb!"

"O–kay." She seems a tad overexcited about this, but whatever, it's Letty. I try to picture him. Will he be more like Alex or more like Ken? Or a strange blend of the two, like chocolate and chili?

She bestows one of her glittering smiles on me. "I can't believe how utterly splendid it is here. You're a genius, Hayley."

"I hope the public sees it the same way." I cock my head to the far room. "That's where we'll start. What do you think?"

"Yes ..." Letty trails off. But if I were seeing all this for the first time, I suppose I'd be speechless too. If it's an indication of how mesmerizing my exhibition is, then I should have nothing to worry about.

"The inaugural tour starts next Thursday."

"Hmm?" Letty scans the room, runs a finger along the red ropes.

"We open next Thursday."

"Oh, Hayley ..." Her eyes narrow as if in pain.

"What?"

"There's no way that Seb is going to allow the public to set foot into this room or any other in this basement."

It's like a blow to the back of my skull with a heavy, blunt instrument. "E–excuse me?"

She nods. "He's in the drawing room. But leave all that to Alex."

No sooner has she backed off than she comes rushing forward to me again, grasping my hands in hers. "Oh, poor Hayley, this is so unfair. He didn't give you any warning, did he? So typical Alex, gambling on the best of all worlds."

When she's gone, I numbly sift through what I know. And the main point is this: Alex is the boss around here. I need to find him. I need to find Alex and sort this bullshit out.

I don't need to go far. He's halfway down the corridor already when I poke my head out the door.

I pull him in, my fists grabbing his shirt. "Letty told me Seb's home."

"Yeah." He runs his hands over my shoulders, up and down. "I was coming to get you."

"And something about him not wanting the gallery open."

"He's not keen on the idea." Alex pauses. I can tell he's choosing his words carefully.

"But it doesn't matter, does it?" I prompt him.

"We may need to"—he winces—"slow down on the whole idea. I'm so sorry, Hayley."

"Why is everyone saying sorry?" My pitch rises to a screech. "By slow down, do you mean *forget* about?"

His eyes search my face. "Ye–ah, it would be best, on the whole. Or at least until we have him on board, and knowing him, it could take weeks."

My palms shoot up to block him off. "Weeks? No. Out of the question, Alex. We put too much into this. Isn't it a cornerstone of your business plan? Isn't that what you told me?"

"Yes, I meant all of that."

"Then why listen to Seb? He hasn't been here. Why are you even considering his opinion?"

Alex's face is rigid, like someone else is pressing a remote control and telling him how to move and what to say. "Hayley, don't make this any more difficult than it already is."

I exhale loudly. "I'm just trying to understand. Are you backing out because you think it's a gamble that won't work? If it is, then why don't you just say it to my face? I'm a big girl. I can handle it."

"That's not it at all. I want the gallery open, too. But Seb's the boss now. You just have to accept it."

This makes absolutely no sense to me. I prowl in a semicircle around him, unable to keep my limbs still. "Last time I checked, you were the duke."

"I'm the bearer of the title."

"Fine. So who is Seb to challenge your plans?"

He presses his lips together. "My brother."

"So?"

"He's got the power."

"Am I misunderstanding something?"

Alex slumps against the wall. He looks pale, like the life has been sucked out of him. "You have to understand, Hayley. The dukedom is rightfully Seb's—morally, ethically, and meritocratically, any way you choose to look. But by accident of birth, it fell to me. It's not Seb's fault he had a different mother. He's had punishment enough."

I'm struggling to get my head around this, not the story itself, but the fact that Alex kept this all from me. "And you were going to tell me all this … when?"

"I didn't know if he'd ever come back, Hayley. I was waiting to find out—"

"If he was still alive?" I finish for him.

"That was one option. The other was that he might not want to resume his position here. But now that he's safely home and anxious to power forward, I'm prepared to get out of his way. I owe him, Hayley."

I fight to catch my breath. Of course, he owes me nothing. Less than nothing. The debt is all on my side. I don't even have the right to be angry, although it doesn't stop the red mist from clouding over my vision. "Then you won't want me here. I'm just in the way."

"Rubbish, Hayley. We'll have more time now … for us."

The conviction I so badly need is missing from his words and from his voice. I try to picture the scenario for a few seconds, but hanging around here for the rest of the semester break, not knowing the fate of the gallery, is not my idea of sanity. And deep down, my secret fantasy of staying on even longer has disintegrated into dust.

"Aren't you happy?" Alex asks, his eyes searing into me.

"Would you be, if you were me?" I snap back. "All my work, for nothing? All your family secrets?"

I've got him. He can't even hold my gaze. I'm right and yet, he doesn't even have the grace to reconsider. "So you're just a puppet duke now, is that it?"

No answer.

"Well, there's no point in dragging this one out. I may as

well go book my flight."

"Hayley—"

"No, Alex." I turn away from him and stride toward the door. I can't bear the expression on his face, the pained glint in his eyes, like he's bottling up something explosive. I'm half expecting him to shout out something as I press down on the handle, but he doesn't, and so I keep going until there's a door between us, and then several more. Each step I take deepens the wound. Soon there'll be eight time zones between us and what will that feel like?

## 27

HAYLEY

"Mara, I am so done playing Cinderella." I'm viciously stuffing clothes into my suitcase while Skyping. "First guy I get serious with and I start to believe in the happy ever after and all the rest of it. What is wrong with me? Fuck him."

I toss another pair of socks into my suitcase on the bed. "Can you believe it? Throwing it all up in the air once his long–lost brother returns, like it was all some kind of experiment. But it's my life we're talking about."

Mara shakes her head in the Skype window. "You let your guard down. We all do it, hun. Try to forgive yourself, if not him."

"Oh, Mara. I wish you were here. You'd see why it's so easy to get swept off your feet."

"Except, it wasn't all imaginary, was it? You got great experience. You made serious connections with interested buyers. This will help your career."

"Maybe I don't want help. Because see where taking shortcuts gets me."

"That was no shortcut. You were working your ass off, girl. You couldn't have possibly known the situation with his brother."

"Unless of course he'd told me," I grumble.

"Okay, yeah. But I do believe Alex would have opened that gallery if Seb hadn't come home."

"Sure, but it's all hypothetical. Bottom line is, I can't trust him to stand up for what he believes in."

"Yeah, that's not good."

We both sigh simultaneously.

"Well," Mara says. "I'll have my phone by me until you reach Heathrow. Call me if you feel even slightly inclined to cave in and go back to him?"

I laugh bitterly. "There's no danger of that. At least I can make decisions and stick to them."

There's a low, impatient–sounding rap on the door.

I jump. "Oh my God, if he's come to try to make me change my mind, I swear I'll strangle him with these bra straps."

Mara's biting her knuckles. "You gonna open?"

"Hold on a sec." I toss the bra into the suitcase.

When I open up, it's a good–looking man I've never seen before ... tall, late twenties or early thirties, black silk shirt and black jeans, shaggy black hair with mini sideburns that actually suit him, pale skin, sensual eyes, and a natural air of superiority about him, someone you wouldn't mess with. Still, I'm in no mood to be nice to anyone, no matter how imposingly they present themselves.

He swivels his head to take in the mess, the suitcase, the laptop screen with the open–mouthed Mara staring out of it.

"You must be Hayley." He's got that same entitled, clipped accent as the rest of them. It's got to be Seb.

Instinctively, I step back and let him wander in. At the center of the room, he cocks his head, looking at me with the most intense, mournful, eyes, that vaguely remind me of El Greco paintings. "I'm Sebastian Belgrave."

No shit. "Hello."

He glances around the room, making me feel like I've stolen something. Perhaps this is meant to be his bedroom? Well, he's welcome to it in about two hours when I'm out of here and after the housekeeper has vacuumed away all traces of my riff–raff self.

His gaze lands on the laptop and lingers. "Who's that?"

"Mara. My friend."

It's almost comical. Separated by 5000 miles, Mara and Seb are wearing the exact same haughty expression on their faces as they stare at each other. Under happier circumstances, I might even introduce them to each other, but as things are, I stay glaring at him, tapping my foot.

"Are you leaving?" His gaze moves to the suitcase and back to my face. He's like a slow–motion version of Alex.

I nod briefly. Why acknowledge out loud what's plain to see? Besides, I can't trust my voice to hold out anymore. I kind of hate Seb for doing whatever he did to turn Alex into a big old coward. I don't have a big brother so maybe I don't understand, but Alex didn't even put up a token fight for me, for us.

"Look, I realize this must be … sudden for you." Seb's voice has softened to a low rumble but is still perfectly audible in the deathly silence. His gaze moves to the window and a wistful expression creeps into his dark eyes. "Alex did well. He did his best. But…"—and now he's frowning—"It's harvest time. We have a backlog, arrears in payments, legislation changes, two tenants' bankruptcies, and a tax deadline. I can't dump all that on Alex and live with myself. It was a mistake to do so and I'm back now to make up for it. I may be paying for it for a very long time."

I squirm, not sure what he wants to hear. Alex never seemed interested in those things.

Then in a brighter voice he says, "But you're perfectly welcome to stay."

"No, thanks." I flash him a tight smile.

He nods solemnly at me, then at Mara on my laptop, and in four brisk strides he's gone, closing the door behind him.

I flop down on the bed and hold my knees, rocking back and forth. Under her mop of auburn hair, I notice Mara's deathly pale. The usual, sassy, pink flush is leached from her cheeks. I've never seen her so dumbstruck.

Neither of us speaks.

"Holy crap," she says finally. "Well if that isn't the most beautiful man I've ever seen then my name's not Mara Madison. It's like they're laying out the temptations in a row, trying to entice you to stay."

I give a hollow laugh. "I must be immune, because all I want to do is get out of here."

"You're still in shock," Mara says.

I force myself to get to work again, squashing down my packed clothes so I can get the suitcase shut. "Let's look on the bright side. With all the excitement of him being back, they'll hardly notice I'm gone."

"All right. Just come home, Hayley," Mara says softly. "We need you here."

## 28

ALEX

I catch seb coming out of Hayley's room. Yes, I've been prowling around trying to figure out what to do, keeping guard like a goddamn Buckingham Palace sentry guard.

"What did you say to her?" I growl, falling in step beside him.

He holds up his palms. "Nothing."

"Nothing?"

"Nothing much. There'll be more arm candy, Alex. Girls love pilots."

I give him my meanest glare.

"No point looking for anything more until it's time to actually get serious. Enjoy your freedom now that you're unshackled."

"Funny, I never considered myself shackled." Everything Seb says is having the reverse effect on me. It makes me want to hold on to Hayley even tighter. It makes me want to be shackled, to wrench back my share of the responsibility he's stolen so easily from me. "Maybe you're the one who needs to loosen up."

Seb–style, he lets my comments linger in the air, somehow rebuking me with his silence. He's always had great command over silences. Maybe I should learn that little trick too. Maybe

I'd get into less trouble then.

We continue walking down the hall. I'm stewing. I'd believed for a precious moment that I had it all, a dukedom, a family business with the potential to thrive, a beautiful, spirited, talented lady by my side.

Goddamn fairy tale.

Mother comes out of the kitchen and glides toward us. Tears gather behind her eyes that have been dry for the entire two months of Seb's absence. "I'm so glad you're back, my dear."

I take the opportunity and dash upstairs, extracting myself from the Seb Appreciation Society. Back in my empty bedroom, I set up watch by the window where I can see any cars coming or going. Every inch of my flesh is craving to go to her room, to beg her to stay and persuade her we'll work it out somehow, but who am I kidding? She's lost all interest in me now that I have no power. She made it abundantly clear.

Soon enough, half an hour later, a gray taxi rolls up to the guest entrance. I watch numbly as the driver puts Hayley's suitcase in the boot and Hayley gets in, huddled under her coat to avoid the drizzle. The whole sequence is dreamlike. I have to convince myself it's real. My heart's so leaden, I'm not sure it's even beating.

Down below, her little face is visible as a white blob through the drizzle–splattered back window of the taxi. I think she's looking right up at me, but from this distance, it's hard to tell.

I don't wave. I don't move a muscle. I don't even breathe. Whatever I'm feeling, I've never felt it before, and it's too overwhelming to put a name to it.

I spring up, my body taking over where my brain left off. She can't leave. I can't let her. Not like this. I bound down the corridor, down the stairs and out the main door before I stop to draw my next breath. My heart's pounding in my ears. The engine's running but the taxi hasn't left yet.

My hand stretches out as I bound across the gravel driveway towards the car. The driver gets the message, nodding. Slowing to a fast walk, I approach Hayley's door. Her face appears at the window, eyes wide in astonishment. Her window lowers half way and she peers at me over the glass.

"You can't leave," I gasp.

She looks away, her forehead tensed up with some emotion I can't read.

"Come on out," I coax.

She shakes her head. The window lowers another few inches, which gives me a little hope, but then she lets out a long sigh of utter resignation. "Alex, I need to get home. You need to work with your brother and sort things out here. We can...we can stay in touch."

I know from the way she's saying it that this is bullshit. "Why? Why did you listen to him?" I growl.

"He sounds like he knows what he's doing."

Her words knock the wind out of me. Speechless, I study her face for signs that this isn't what I think it is—a quality judgement on me. But her normally soft eyes are hard, her mouth a thin, determined line. She's folding her arms and cocking her head backwards in a gesture that's so Seb–like, it's clear he's just recruited himself a new disciple.

"So, that's it then?" I say, kicking the gravel under my shoe. "Not interested in someone who's only second–in–command?"

"Believe it or not, this isn't about your ego, Alex."

"What then?" I yell. But I know it's the wrong answer. And I'll be damned if I can think of the correct one. I can't save this situation. She's determined to go.

Without another word, her window rolls up. My stomach clenches with regret and self–loathing.

When the taxi disappears into the sycamores surrounding our front gates, I drag myself back to my room, root out my wallet, pull out my British Airways black card and call the special services number.

It's the least I can do.

29

HAYLEY

The tears I allowed myself to shed in the taxi have dried up pretty quickly in the hustle and bustle that is the emigration procedure in Heathrow. Nothing soothes the tender feelings of a broken heart quite like squeezing along in a foul–smelling line and being barked at to remove your shoes, empty your pockets, and hold your arms up like you're surrendering to a firing squad. I guess I'll have plenty of time later to mope. My whole life, actually.

When I arrive at my gate, there's yet another document check. By this stage, I'm rendered docile—Heathrow has officially broken me. I fish my documents out of my purse for the fourth time.

The über–poised British Airways gate agent pauses after reading my name. I'm ready to throttle her if there's been any mistake, or problem, or if I'm one of those passengers they're going to politely ask to give up their places because it's an overbooked flight. Because I won't do it.

"Ms. Cochrane, you've received an upgrade."

"Are you serious?" I blink a few times. "Upgrade to—?"

"A first–class seat, madam." Her smile is functional. "4A."

"Wow." A vision of one of those huge, comfy airline chairs that expands into a bed floats before my eyes. Not even Uncle Stig managed that on our trip over with his magic diplomatic passport, though he did try. "How?"

"I don't have that information, madam." Her tone says, Move along please. Stop asking these questions and just count yourself lucky.

"Thank you." I grab my suitcase handle and maneuver myself away to let the next traveler in.

It's not until I'm easing back in my massive, beige, faux–leather seat in 4A with a glass of champagne and a groan of relief that it strikes me. This was Alex.

Despite myself, a little smile overtakes my face. Then the guilt sets in. This satisfaction with the trappings of prestige is what got me into trouble in the first place. These easy conveniences of power that are susceptible to the whims of the upper class. I need to be strong and rise above the temptations of easy solutions if I'm going to be an authentic artist. I need to be independent. I should have refused the seat to make a point.

But as I sink into the pillow and stretch out my legs, I know I'm just going to go along with it because I probably can't change it anyway and it feels too damn good to be able to rest my head on a flight.

It's his last point. His last power display. Classy, playful, and utterly luxurious. Fine, he wins.

# 30

ALEX

September has arrived and the estate is turning shades of copper and gold. It's been a whole month since Hayley's departure. I haven't had the will to go to London and get laid, which is my usual cure for the blues. I haven't had the will to go anywhere and get laid. Even Ken thinks this is a long stretch and he tried to set me up with one of his female jockey types. I only went so as not to hurt his feelings. The date was polite, efficient and, ultimately, a dud.

After Hayley left, I draped dust covers over the paintings the way she showed me and they're still there. I check my phone for the hygrometer settings from the smart aircon and dehumidifier. It's part of my daily routine before I start work. Seb continues to resist the idea that selling them is something worth investigating. I think it's a matter of pride for him that the farm should be our main source of income. That's another thing he has in common with Mother. He only likes the outside of buildings, and gardens. He doesn't like being indoors much. He'd let this lot rot before he even realized it was wasting away.

I have to admit our daily grind is easier with Seb around. The man's a machine, pounding in overtime hours, like the maniac he is, to have things the way he wants them. He reports with ruthless efficiency to the tenants and expects the same from them. Despite their grumbling, they're visibly relieved that he's back, constantly scouring for new suppliers, new growth techniques, new markets. The paperwork backlogs have cleared. The desks and in–trays have been conquered. I'm doing my bit, drifting from task to task, taking orders from above.

Mother floats around the castle grounds with the hint of a smile on her face. She's taken to wearing brighter colors. And I don't hear Ken or Letty complaining much either. Ken's evenings are no longer taken up with my mad schemes, so he's free to go back to his horses. Letty's often with him when she's not doing her music lessons. I'm back to flying again. It's amazing how everything drifts back to how it was before.

But I see the dangers, too, stuff I was blind to before. Seb is heading for a breakdown. He's torn between his desire to have control and the fact that he's getting no credit publicly for anything. The public and our group of friends have started to see me as someone who might actually have a serious opinion from time to time. I'm getting inquiries addressed to me about the farm that I have to hide from him. Sometimes I have to do copious research just so my answers don't sound dumb.

And there are moments when I sense Seb's sadness. I've caught him gazing at architectural projects online when he thinks no one is looking—restoration projects where they create beautiful new living spaces from old stone buildings. He's got something in mind for the dilapidated eighteenth century houses at the western section of our estate, or would, if it weren't for his crushing workload.

I indulge in acts of rebellion to let off steam. For example, today, I get to chauffeur His Royal Highness the Saudi Prince from Kent to Oxford. It's my first attempt to earn money by myself, on my own terms, doing something I actually understand—and I'm kind of excited about it.

Just as I'm about to jump in the Aston Martin to go to the

airfield, Seb comes wandering up. He tilts his head back and to the left, a signal of disapproval he's not even aware of making. "The prince?"

I nod at my gear in the passenger seat and slide into the driver seat.

"I'm surprised you're doing it."

"Are you?" I say sarcastically.

"Isn't chauffeuring a menial occupation for a duke?"

I give him a cheesy grin just to piss him off and slide on my aviator sunglasses. "Good enough for me." I've decided to see where I can take this as a business and like it or not, I'll be transporting people far less salubrious than a crown prince. So fuck Seb.

I lean out the window in case my brother has any brilliant parting words of wisdom before I drive off. He just raises his forefinger to his forehead in a mock salute. That, I suppose, would be his brilliant word of wisdom.

"See you later." I screech backward over the gravel stones, making sure to cover his shoes in dust.

# 31

ALEX

The prince and I are flying at two thousand feet over rolling Oxford countryside. In Oxford, there's a pub called the Mason's Arms, which has its own helipad. They're letting me use it for a cut in the deal. A criminally generous cut—to ensure absolute discretion. But that's how it works. From there, there's a private car to pick up His Majesty.

"Are you excited about getting married?" I ask in Arabic as we sit at the window of the pub after a smooth landing, drinking tea. I've been practicing the fiendishly difficult language every day with a tutor. I'm bloody–minded enough to want to get it right this time.

"Oh yes. Raihana is beautiful. Raihana is my third wife."

I give him an indulgent smile. I know better than to ask about the first two, or anything about that situation. Juggling several wives must be a complicated business and I don't envy him. I'm thinking of a remark to make about the weather when he pipes up again.

"Why are you single?" he asks.

I laugh. "I'm enjoying my freedom."

"Will you wait for long?"

I shrug. There's no easy answer. Especially when my mind is so taken up with one person who seems impossibly far away in every sense.

The prince gazes at me. "My first wife, Malea, I married her when I was twenty." The prince has switched to English. "The Council advised me to marry her to smooth my path to the throne. At one stage my father preferred me to become heir, but there was a hitch: I had three brothers senior to me."

I whistle appreciatively.

He lets out a laugh. "Also five half–brothers, and four cousins, all with an equal claim to the throne." He pauses. "You've heard the stories, no? It's been all over the news at home. One had to be bribed off to step aside. Another was declared insane, a third is in disgrace, charged with murdering the oil minister."

The prince continues and the names and the methods for knocking them all off become a jumble of Arabic names to me. "Yes, my sudden rise upset many branches of the royal family, but for the time being"—he grins, showing a mouthful of perfect white teeth— "I am fifth in line."

"Sounds complicated," I say.

The prince stirs his tea with a delicate silver spoon. "In our Bedouin system, the whole family gets together in a committee to decide the succession. There's too much at stake with fluctuating oil prices and the dangerous political muddle in the region. In the wrong hands, the entire kingdom could return to its desert roots."

"Monarchies are complicated," I say, even though the British system is kindergarten compared to the Saud dynasty, not to mention virtually powerless.

"And your own duchy?" he asks.

"Everything goes to the firstborn, legitimate male, and there's only one wife to produce the offspring. As long as there's male issue at all, it's usually uncomplicated."

He nods. "Yes, as in your case."

"Well, I feel my brother got passed over, because on merit, the title should be his."

The prince looks at me uncomprehendingly. "What is this

merit you speak of?"

"He's cleverer, harder working …"

The prince throws back his head and laughs.

I wait politely.

"A man has been charged with murder," he says, "another shut away in an asylum all in order that I gain two steps up in the line of succession. And you talk about guilt?" His beady, black eyes drill into me with conviction. "Every day of my life, I live with this guilt. But I cannot let that trip me up. I will not let bitter curses and threats stop me from doing what is right, striving for my place if I am needed."

"Threats to kill you?"

He acknowledges with slowly lowered eyelids.

We leave the pub in silence and I'm chewing on this information as we walk towards the helicopter. The prince suddenly says, "So, my dear cousin, I am afraid I cannot even begin to understand how you can shy away from your advantageous birth circumstances and your responsibility."

"I don't expect you to understand," I say, as we reach the helicopter.

Because the truth is, I don't understand it either. And I haven't understood it since a certain person came into my life and showed me who I could be and that it involves so much more than an accident of birth, an antiquated title, or a cloak and coronet. It involves believing in myself. I *am* the rightful heir and I'm ready to prove it.

## 32

HAYLEY

I'm sitting on the porch with Dad in our favorite spot to watch the sunset. A gentle breeze is blowing. Sitting at my workbench, I'm preparing canvases for two oil paintings. Dad's fixing fishing lines, which are strewn out over the coffee table in the cozy corner. I watch him fondly. He's been a great support this past month as I moped my way through the rest of the holidays before the semester. He never asked for explanations, which is just as well as I wasn't prepared to give any. Full days have gone by where I've hardly spoken a word to anyone except Mara.

Just as I've stuck in the last pin into the wooden frame, Dad, who's been watching me the whole time, says, "Maybe it's time you told me about Alex?"

I snap my box of pins shut. "There's not much to know."

He leans in, hand on one knee. "Hayley, you don't call your father and tell him you're not coming home for two months for no reason. You don't wander around like you've left half your brain somewhere else. Maybe I've no right to know, but I sure am interested."

I wriggle among the cushions, trying to find a comfortable position.

"Is he special?"

"Yes. He is." I let out a long sigh. "Or, was."

Dad's waiting, so I continue. "I didn't like the situation … in the end. But before that it was great because we were a team, building something new. Making a difference. Until we weren't."

"You sound so much like your mother just now."

I flush with pleasure. "I do?"

"Yes." Dad fiddles with his fishing line some more and after completing a new hook, he catches my gaze.

"She'd never have let this happen to her," I say glumly. "She'd have made that gallery a huge success somehow."

Dad winces. "Maybe it's time I stopped sugarcoating the folklore about your mother's side of the family."

I look at him curiously.

"Yes, Hayley. As a single woman, your mother was controlled by her father and her brothers and she had no say in what happened in her life. There's just no way to gloss over some of the things Grandpa did in the name of his business—extortion and blackmail were only part of it. Your mother needed to get away from that, but Grandpa was reluctant to release her from the back–office work."

"So, you married her and she became an independent artist and bought her own studio." I finish the familiar tale for him.

Dad shakes his head slowly. "She had her own studio, alright, but I bought that for her with the money I'd saved up to start my own fish farm."

"Oh. But she earned it back, right?"

"Not exactly." His chin muscles bunch up with the grim reality of it. "She never earned a penny with her art."

I get a fluttery feeling in my belly.

"No, that's not true. She sold it all."

Dad winces. "That's where the truth might have been glossed over. Not to say her painting weren't good," Dad continues. "They were. But when nobody wanted it commercially after showing it around for three years, well, she went a little mad and she ended up destroying it." He laughs softly to himself as if caught in a memory. "She had some temper."

"She didn't sell anything?" I ask, my voice croaking.

"No, she took it all down in a bundle to the back of the garden and made a bonfire out of it. The canvases, the drawing pads, the wooden sculptures, all of it. There was nothing left. Just charcoal. She was devastated afterward. So was I. So, I worked twice as hard to get a promotion with the fish factory."

"Which you hated," I say in wonder.

Dad's eyes soften. "Oh, I was in love, so that didn't matter. And then of course, you were on the way. You saved her."

I shake my head, not wanting to be lured by this surprising twist. "So, she was always dependent on you?"

"In many ways, but I on her, too. Hayley, and that's normal when it comes to the ones we love." Dad smiles wistfully. "It's not such a bad thing, is it?"

I massage the side of my head. "I don't know."

"I've kept the peace over the years by staying quiet—too quiet. I shouldn't have, Hayley. It's nothing but a disservice to you, but your uncle Stig, he's always been so attentive to you and he's the nearest relative to your mother that you've got, so I let him feed you his sanitized view of his family. He insisted you needed a strong female role model."

"I thought you'd stolen away her dreams … but you actually gave her the freedom she needed, and she blew it?"

Dad grins ruefully. "I don't see it that way at all. I just wish the fishing business had been more profitable and I could offer you better financial support, Hayley, that's the biggest regret of my life. But there's one thing I will offer you, and that's the blessing to follow your heart wherever it may take you."

"Oh, Dad." I sink into him and he wraps his sinewy arms around me. I can't believe I've underestimated him so terribly.

He draws back. "What do you want to do?"

I straighten my legs in front of me, hesitant to share, but

then I give in. "I've come to a realization over the summer. Maybe it's from studying too much art, from being surrounded by the true artists' work every day from dusk till dawn. Maybe it's from having to articulate it to Alex what made these paintings special and finding myself tongue–tied at times. The thing is, I'm not good enough to go it alone as an artist. I just don't have that ... that *depth*."

"Hayley—"

My palm flies up. "No, it's okay, Dad, just listen. This may sound crazy, but I think I've inherited your business sense more than you think. I know I can make this work. Maybe not with Belgrave Castle, but with other private collections. This is what excites me, helping people discover the value of their collections. The logistics of setting up the show. And showing those collections to people who've never studied art. Networking. It's not such a dirty word."

His brows furrow and unfurrow and furrow again, like a stage curtain to his soul. "Are you sure?"

"Yes. I'm going to start small, on the side, while I finish my studies. I'll start by offering consultancy services to collectors and owners."

What I don't mention is that my assets are just about large enough to buy a bag of horse fodder for Frodo the pony in the Belgrave stables. It's pathetic. It's one thing to want it, and say it, it's another thing to figure out the how and by that, I mean the financials. For starters, I need a web designer, a personal assistant, gas money. "It might take a while to get up and running." I say, not wanting to spell out the cash flow complications.

"What about this duke? Didn't he offer you that exact job?"

I let out a hollow laugh. "That bridge is well burned."

"Pity."

"I know," I groan. "But Dad, I can't go back. Alex's isn't even the boss anymore. It's Seb, his brother. Alex let his power go just as quickly as he let me go. He's on to the next shiny thing by now, I expect."

Dad pauses to examine my face. "Did you talk to the new guy?"

"Seb? No. I should have fought for it, but Alex told me not to." I sigh. "I blew it, so let's not talk about it again."

## 33

ALEX

The last guests depart from the castle. Mother heaves a sigh of relief as she locks the main door. "That's it for another fortnight."

Seb removes the rope barricade from the doorway of the dining room. "Just a week, Mother. I'm opening the doors next Saturday again."

She gives a precise, little shudder that seems designed to elevate our blood pressures.

I step forward. "We can postpone for a month. Two even. If we just open the gallery."

"Alex, no," Seb mutters. "It's been a long day. Mother's tired."

"Let me sell the Lillienthal collection then. Just that. Collectors are interested. Hayley was right."

"I really don't think—"

"Look, Seb. I love that you're back, I really do, but here's the thing, we made some changes around here while you were gone. Good ones. Yes, it was chaotic, and yes, we all sacrificed our free time and our hobbies to do it. But we managed it, and we learned a lot. And Hayley—she figured out what's worth selling and what's worth keeping from Father's mess. We need extra cash fast, so why not at least give my idea a chance?"

"Heaven's above," Mother whimpers. "Are you talking about selling again?"

Seb goes over to comfort her, draping his arm around her shoulder. I glare at them both. She responds with her tragic look. Seb looks like he's been carved from stone except for his eyes darting between Mother and me. This is the point at which I'd normally cave in.

"What do you really care? You haven't even set foot in there in a decade, have you?" I demand. "Either of you." My angry voice echoes off the polished surfaces of the hall. Mother shrinks further into Seb.

He shakes his head. "And I don't intend to."

"Well, that's a pity. Did you know there's an early Zeta–Clarke there and a Rory Hamilton sketch? One of his sold for half a million last year. Not even the Tate can compete with our collection of sketches by Grainger. We could host tours on seven separate themes—yes, seven. We could earn more money from one wall in seconds than with an entire season of open days."

I'm amazed at how Hayley-like I sound now.

Seb flashes a condescending smile. "It's not the money—"

"I beg to differ, Seb," I interrupt before he can continue with some crap about preserving Father's things and that selling off assets is not a noble way to make money. "My proposal is we reduce the number of public days to zero, and make up the rest with the gallery and with my helicopter rides. Take it or leave it."

"Helicopter rides?" Mother clutches her stomach as if in pain.

"For people who value privacy and class. I have the experience, the connections, and the cash to make it work."

I turn to my brother. "Seb, which is more important? That we preserve our ancestral home, this beautiful estate and its heritage buildings that have been in our family for hundreds of years? Or that we hang on to a bunch of paintings we've owned for less than a generation? I know it's been your dream to renovate the cottages at the village end of the estate, but you've never had time. Well, let me do this and you'll have the time to follow your dream. Don't even bother trying to deny it."

He flinches and breaks eye contact. I have him. If he's stupid enough to argue, I'll tell him I've seen his printouts of the ground plan shoved under purchase orders in his in tray. Hell, I'll run and fetch them as evidence.

"But you know nothing about art," he says.

"I know a bit. And I can get help."

He plants his hands on his hips. "And if I say no?"

I step toward him. "Then I will use my power as duke to overrule you. If that means taking you to court and calling in security, then by God, I will!"

"Alex!" Mother's hand flies to her mouth.

Seb pales. "What's gotten into you? I—I don't know you."

"Are you in or not?" I demand.

"In? In what?" Seb says with cold fury. "What about that bullshit you fed me? You wanted your life back. Well, I gave it to you."

"And are you happy?" I ask.

Scorn is written all over his face. "All I know is I'll be the one picking up the pieces when your next woman comes along."

"Wrong answer, Seb. So, let me reiterate. Are you happy?"

He releases Mother and steps closer. "If you wanted the dukedom, then why didn't you say so? I'd have gone on a different path."

"I felt I owed it to you."

He scoffs. "Pity, huh?" He rocks his weight from foot to foot as if he's deciding which angle to lunge at me from. "God, Alex."

"More like guilt," I mutter, just loud enough for him, but not Mother, to hear.

"I can't believe I'm hearing this. You know what? Do what you like." He jabs his finger at my chest. "You're the duke. Not me. You."

He turns and stomps down the east wing, Mother scuttling after him. I'm stunned. Seb's never given in before, and it sure doesn't feel like victory. But underneath my amazement and anxiety over what he's going to do next, another feeling struggles for attention, one so alien to me I hardly recognize it at first: relief.

I'm done with the pretense, the veneer of the cocky duke, the playboy duke. I can't change the laws of primogeniture. I can't undo the cruel way Seb was disillusioned by our parents. But I can face up to the consequences of their actions. I'm ready to be duke and to protect the endangered species I belong to. I have everything I need to achieve this.

Well, almost everything. The key ingredient is missing.

# 34

HAYLEY

I finish sharpening my 6B pencil and blow away the wood shavings. The nude model wriggling on the stage is new. His eyes dart around our semicircle in embarrassment, telling me the poor dude has never done this before.

I drop my gaze to my sheet of paper to make it easier for him until he gets into it. It usually takes five minutes for the nervousness of the novice models to relax into boredom. I couldn't strip naked in front of twenty–four students, but he must have decided the money was worth it.

It's then I become aware of the whir–whir of chopper blades very near, nearer than I've ever heard them in school.

All eyes gravitate to the window, where an airbus helicopter is hovering a hundred yards away. A military drill? Or is there a dignitary at the school today? I heard nothing about it. And it's not like Canterbury College is even Oregon's finest school, or even in the top ten.

"They've landed on the basketball court," Cary Smith says in wonder as the noise dies down.

"That's unorthodox," Professor Moines, our teacher, says. "But students, poor Mr. Sanchez is only here for another ten minutes. Let's make the most of it."

I look back to our slightly shivering model. I'm sure the professor didn't mean to say "poor" but yeah, poor Mr. Sanchez still looks as uncomfortable as ever, scratching his arm even though he's not supposed to be moving. I guess he has something interesting to watch out the window now.

I'm half–heartedly shading in the shadows under the pathetic muscles where his six pack should be when there's a rap on the classroom door.

As the door opens, my head springs up and it's the person I least expect to see.

Alex.

My pencil drops from my fingers and clatters to the floor.

He strolls right in, easy as you please, and yet there's that ineffable air of superiority and authority about him, like a rooster among chickens. He gives Mr. Sanchez an ironic wave.

I'm stunned and can only look on like a zombie as he stands there. My fellow students, mostly female, sit up straighter and fingers reach up to preen faces and hair. All eyes have moved from the nude model to Alex. I remove my hand from where I've clasped it over my mouth and attempt a smile, but I can't be sure if it's working or not.

"Excuse me." Professor Moines gives him a steely look over her glasses. "But who are you?"

"Begging your pardon. I'm Alex. I've just come to get Hayley." His voice is smooth, unwavering, and totally out of place here in this classroom.

All heads turn to me at warp speed. I can only absorb their curiosity in stricken silence, unable to move or think. All I seem able to do is breathe rapidly and stare at him, my beautiful duke.

"Is that your helicopter?" Professor Moines demands.

"That's correct."

"Do you have permission to land there?"

"Madam, I assure you, it's fine." Alex approaches me slowly, now with a razor–sharp focus on my face.

I'm a complete mess. I almost wish he'd go away, that this strange thing is not happening. Because I can't deal with it.

"Come with me?" he asks, reaching out his hand. His gaze is unblinking, his cheeks glowing.

My hands stay clasped together on my drawing pad. "You could have just called." I hate that it comes out as a breathy squeal, several tones higher than usual.

"Yeah, I don't trust you with phones."

There's a curve to his lip, a so–familiar gesture that seems etched in my heart. It jolts me awake enough to take his warm hand in mine. Oh, it feels like heaven. Memories flood back when our fingers entwine.

There's a collective sigh from my fellow students as I follow Alex out the classroom door, like in a fairy tale, I suppose.

But as we get out to the corridor alone, my wits return to their full capacity. I make a sign that we should go into the next empty classroom, 10–D. I am so going to give this cocky duke a piece of my mind.

I follow him into the classroom and watch as he takes up a spot in front of the whiteboard, like a teacher. Who does he think he is? He must sense I'm going to explode because he holds up his palms like a man before a firing squad. I perch on the edge of the front desk, arms folded protectively. This is just too sudden, too unreal, too unexplained.

"I didn't fight for you to stay," he says.

Too damn right you didn't.

"I should have," he adds when I don't reply. "It was what I wanted."

Did he come all this way to torture me with a reminder of his second thoughts? "It was my decision, Alex, and I'm glad you didn't make it harder for me." My voice, though wavering, has at least returned to its normal pitch.

He groans. "But it was the wrong decision, Hayley. Based on the wrong information. You only saw a snapshot of my life, and it was all a pretense. Until it started to become real, that is, and then of course when Seb returned, I wasn't thinking straight. I let guilt take over."

I grimace. "No, Alex, I was the one not thinking straight. I let my plans for the gallery take over everything, including ... us. It was a huge mistake." As I'm saying it, I'm admitting it, to myself, surprising myself.

He comes closer. "You showed me what hard work and taking responsibility can achieve. When you were there, when we were working together, I believed in myself for the first time. I suddenly wanted it all—the stability, the responsibility, a strong, beautiful woman by my side. Hayley, I want a second chance."

His words thaw the ice around my heart. I study the pattern on the parquet floor until I grasp the right words. "And all the time, I was afraid of being controlled. I guess I dumped you in the same category as my uncle and my dad. I couldn't see the real you struggling underneath the pomp, the money, the power." I meet his gaze. "You put Seb on a pedestal and chastised yourself for not being the same as him. You were going through some serious shit. I realize that now."

"And in my hour of weakness, I let you go rather than include you in what was really going on. I had persuaded myself you didn't want me if I didn't have power. But now I realize … it was the dumbest excuse of my life for not stepping up. Because Hayley—"

He walks around the desks and stands chest to chest with me. "I love you. I have since the first day. I should never have let you run away."

My stomach flips at his words.

"I love you too." I run my lips over the stubble of his cheek. He's got a sexy five–o'clock shadow thing going that I never saw in the castle and I think I'm going to ask him to keep it. He shivers as my hands slide under his T–shirt and smooth down his six–pack, edging downward. I want to torture him a little. No, a lot.

"But call off your MI6 thugs," I say when I've made his eyes close in pleasure.

"I'll do better than that: I'll introduce you guys," he groans, grasping my hips and pulling me hard against him so his erection grinds into my belly. "Because Hayley, I can't live another day without you. I don't know how, but we have to be together. I can't give up my dukedom and run away, but I offer you everything in it. Tell me you want it, too."

His expression beseeches me, but the answer comes from my own convictions. "I want it too. Especially this part. And I've got some plans of my own—plans that would involve moving to England—that I think will fit nicely into what you have in mind."

His wolf eyes are ablaze. "All I have in mind right now"— his big hands cradle my chin, his thumbs tracing the outline of my jaw and pressing into the flesh of my cheeks— "is to make love to you in a helicopter."

"What? Have you never fucked in a helicopter?" I tease.

"No. But we can do that too."

His lips crash down on mine, and this time, I know life is going to be great with my cocky duke.

# EPILOGUE
## (A YEAR LATER)

HAYLEY

"Hey, why aren't you getting dressed?" I ask, stalking into our bedroom. It's ten to six, and I'm horribly late for getting ready for dinner, but I'm flush with excitement over selling off the last two Lillienthal portraits for double the sum I was expecting. I can't wait to see their faces when I tell them at dinner. But first of all, I want to make the announcement to my beloved Alex who's helped me all the way, despite his workload in the family business and in his side–business too.

Alex is fiddling with something behind the curtain. He straightens up, guiltily. "There you are."

"What're you up to?" I stride across the carpet and try to see but he holds my wrists tightly, blocking my path.

"Alex, I have to get changed," I protest, trying to wriggle away. "You have to get ...changed." Then I notice he is changed. Very changed. He's wearing his tuxedo—the one that emphasizes his broad shoulders and tapering waist to such a degree that I don't like other women even seeing him in it.

"Are you going somewhere?" I ask.

"That depends."

"On?"

He moves in closer and his lips graze my forehead. "You."

My eyes pop open in surprise. "What?"

There are beads of sweat on his forehead and his eyes waver with an uncertainty I don't think I have ever experienced in him. My throat tightens with anxiety, trying to figure out what's going on. Some royal function where he has to hobnob with a bunch of self–important lords and ladies of the realm? But that would hardly faze him.

"Do I need to change too?" I ask in a small voice.

182

"No, you're just fine. Although…" His eyes roam from my eyes to my stocking feet, "I don't mind if you get naked for this."

"What?"

He squeezes his eyes shut and then open again. He lets out a breath that's almost pained. Then he's lowering himself down to my eye level, then lower, and lower again. It's not the time for a blow job no matter how horny he's making me with this strange act of his. "Alex, I—"

"Shhhh. Look at me, Hayley."

I meet his eyes. And then I see. Oh God, he's on one knee, not two. And yes, he's holding a small box in black velvet. He can't be…he's not…

"Hayley, my love, will you marry me?"

My knees weaken and I crumple down beside him onto the carpet, grasping his fingers in mine. He presses the box into my palm. "What do you say?"

I enclose the box in my fingers, unable to peel my eyes from his face. "Are you serious?"

His lips curl up slightly to one side. "What do you think?"

"Fuck…I mean *yes*," I yell, throwing my arms around his neck, pulling his mouth to mine with my fist still clutching the unopened box. We kiss messily, I'm so out of control, like I'm kissing him for the first time again. Then I kiss him properly, deeply, pouring the tender feelings that have matured over the last twelve months into him. Because we've weathered the distance, the ups and downs, the complexity of family life and castle life and we've always come out stronger. From the very beginning, it's been intense, and a little bit crazy, and we've been forced to find out so much about the other in a short period of time. We've lived through more together than couples who have dated for five years. Marriage will make us stronger again. I just *know*.

"You'll be my duchess?" When he draws back, Alex's face is bathed in smiles he can't control. "My lady Hayley."

"Just Hayley, to you. Everything else sounds so weird. I

don't think I'll ever get used to that aspect of it."

He grins and straightens his bow-tie. "Well Hayley, I'm taking you for a ride to celebrate."

"Where to?"

"London, Paris, Berlin…anywhere within a five–hundred–mile radius because that's as much fuel as will fit in the tank."

"You're taking the chopper?"

"Why not? Time I used it for our fun, not just everyone else's."

I picture Seb's disapproving face when he hears of this. But even Seb can't deny that Alex's helicopter business has turned a tidy three hundred percent profit this year which is more than we can say for the eco–farming business, even if that's a somewhat unfair comparison. "Oh God, that's brilliant! Let's do it."

Laughing, he pulls me into his chest. He's heaving in time with my own rapid breathing. "So, grab your passport, Lady."

But I'm more interested in grabbing him. I let the box fall onto the bed and my hands grapple at his waistband, pulling up the shirt, running my fingers feverishly along the smooth muscle of his lower abdomen.

Alex groans and clutches my hips. "Paris can wait?"

I nod. "Berlin too."

"We'll do the whole damn world on our honeymoon—"

"Oooh, lots of galleries," I murmur.

"And fuck in every capital city."

"You sure are one cocky duke."

He smirks. "I was perfectly innocent until you came along."

While we're laughing, and kissing and getting naked, it becomes clear to me that it doesn't matter where we go or what we do. No gallery or tourist attraction can compete with the sheer feeling of joy that this man brings to my life. We could honeymoon in the castle dungeons and I'd still be happy. Of course, I don't mention this to him in case he thinks it's a great idea and wants to try it for a laugh. Because that would be so Alex.

"Let's worry about the honeymoon later and actually get married first," I suggest as we sink, spent, across the bed after a very fast and wild session of consummating our engagement.

"Soon?" he asks trailing a finger between my breasts.

"Hell, yes."

"Well, it's June now. We've kind of missed the season."

"Season's not over til end of August." I'm easing the ring out if its silky padding in the box now, something I forgot to do in my excitement. Of course it fits perfectly. The big rock glints dazzlingly under the candlelight. The sight of it sitting on my middle finger makes me feel dizzy. It's probably worth more than my father's house back in Laxby and all our belongings inside it.

"Is it okay?"

"That's one word for it."

Alex hooks a finger under my chin, tilting me up to meet his gaze. "Hey, no freaking out on me, all right? A lady needs a ring. Duke's orders."

"Actually, Alex," I lean my cheek into his palm and gaze deeply into his wolf–like eyes. "All I need is you."

# WANT TO KNOW HOW THE SAGA CONTINUES?

Seb's story is next! Yes, you'll find out more about the mysterious older brother who's been AWOL throughout this book. Now that he's back, will he try to grab all power back from Alex and how will all that play out if Alex has a new sense of purpose in his life? Or is it possible that Seb might have *softened*? And if so, who is the woman who's managed to tame him? (Hint: she's someone we know!)

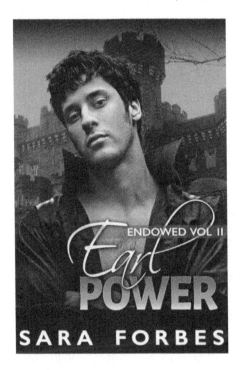

...It's Mara! Yes, Hayley's best friend manages to get sucked into the vortex that is the Belgrave family with all its aristocratic complexity and inter-generational friction. Find out how this unlikely couple meet and enjoy the fireworks that result in two hot-headed characters battling for their rights to be respected by everyone around them...and each other.

So sign up to my email list (over on saraforbes.com) to be the first to get your hands on Seb's story (and all others that follow!). You'll also get discounts and deals.

And finally, if you liked my book please, please, please tell a friend about it. Or a colleague. Or your sister, brother, next-door neighbor. As long as people are reading and loving my books, I'll keep writing them. And don't forget if you want to know how the story continues, check out the second book in the "Endowed" series: Earl Power. It's hot, with a somewhat darker hero, but with all the fun and pomp of the first book!

Please leave a review on Amazon for me telling me your honest thoughts on this book.

Thanks for reading. Readers like you mean everything to me.

Sara x

Made in the USA
Coppell, TX
03 October 2024

38116244R00105